BUZZ AR

They Said It...

"She's not beautiful, but...she's definitely something else. Her hair is as dark as her eyes, and her mouth looks...kissable. I can't fool myself, though. Mattie's determination was inherited directly from her father, a man with a reputation for getting what he wants."

—Detective Lucas Haines

"Lucas wants to deepen his investigation by pretending we're a couple. What choice do I have? I would do a lot more than be seen in his company to avenge Alan Cargill's murder."

—Mattie Clayton

"I know Mattie thinks there is emotional distance between us. But in my heart, she's still my little girl. I'd do anything for her."

—Steve Clayton

"Mattie's relationship with Lucas is good for her. I can see it in her eyes."

—Sophia Grosso Murphy

MARISA CARROLL

is the pen name of sisters Carol Wagner and Marian Franz. They have been writing bestselling books as a team for almost twenty-five years. During that time they have published more than forty titles, many for the Harlequin Superromance line and Feature and Custom Publishing. They are the recipients of several industry awards, including a Lifetime Achievement Award from *RT Book Reviews* and a RITA® Award nomination from Romance Writers of America, and their books have been featured on the *USA TODAY,* Waldenbooks and B. Dalton bestseller lists. The sisters live near each other in northwestern Ohio, surrounded by children, grandchildren, brothers, sisters, aunts, uncles, cousins and old and dear friends.

NASCAR®

INTO THE CORNER

Marisa Carroll

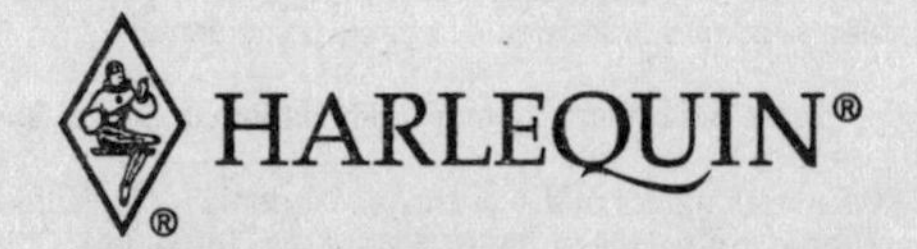

TORONTO • NEW YORK • LONDON
AMSTERDAM • PARIS • SYDNEY • HAMBURG
STOCKHOLM • ATHENS • TOKYO • MILAN • MADRID
PRAGUE • WARSAW • BUDAPEST • AUCKLAND

ISBN-13: 978-0-373-18532-0

INTO THE CORNER

Marisa Carroll is acknowledged as the author of this work.

This edition published by arrangement with Harlequin Books S.A.

www.eHarlequin.com

Printed in U.S.A.

NASCAR HIDDEN LEGACIES

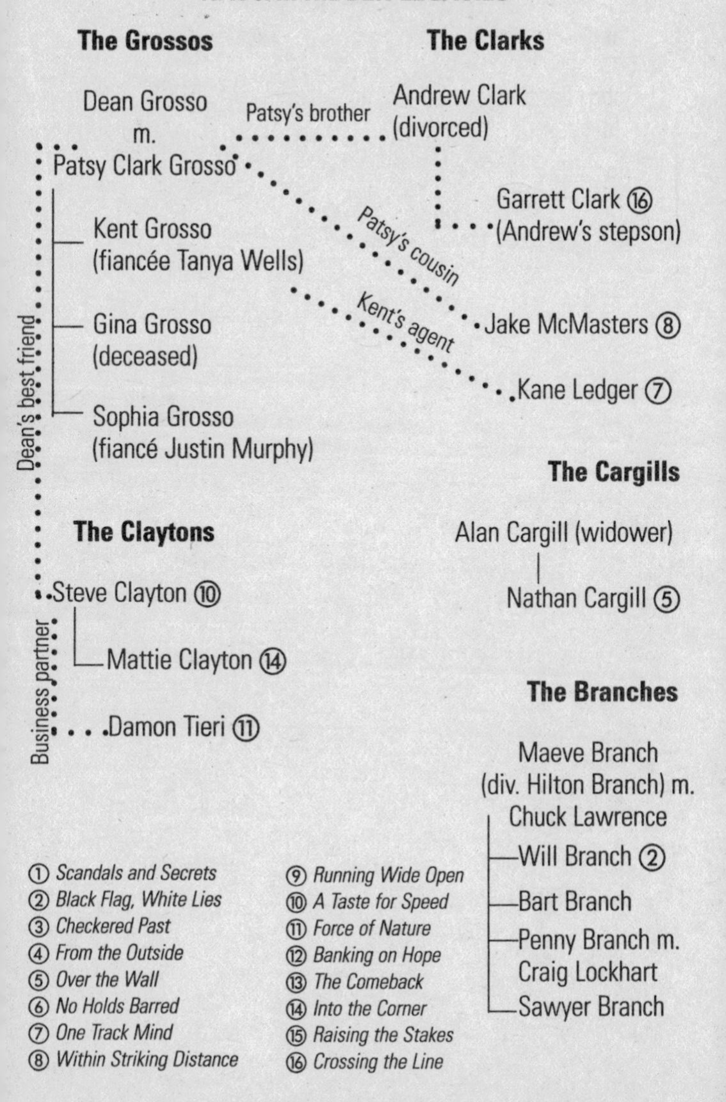

THE FAMILIES AND THE CONNECTIONS

The Sanfords

Bobby Sanford
(deceased)
m.
Kath Sanford

- Adam Sanford ①
- Brent Sanford ⑫
- Trey Sanford ⑨

The Hunts

Dan Hunt
m.
Linda (Willard) Hunt
(deceased)

- Ethan Hunt ⑥
- Jared Hunt ⑮
- Hope Hunt ⑫
- Grace Hunt Winters ⑯
(widow of Todd Winters)

The Mathesons

Brady Matheson
(widower)
(fiancée Julie-Anne Blake)

- Chad Matheson ③
- Zack Matheson ⑬
- Trent Matheson
(fiancée Kelly Greenwood)

The Daltons

Buddy Dalton
m.
Shirley Dalton

- Mallory Dalton ④
- Tara Dalton ①
- Emma-Lee Dalton

CHAPTER ONE

DETECTIVE LUCAS HAINES spotted his quarry at a table outside a wine shop, a snooty, high-end establishment that catered to the Yuppies and academic types that frequented this university neighborhood in a leafy suburb of Charlotte, North Carolina. She'd insisted they meet here, rather than at her apartment two streets over. He didn't mind. It was a prudent thing for a woman living alone to do. He slowed his step for a moment and watched as she sat there, long legs crossed at the knee, her attention claimed by something he couldn't see.

Mattie Clayton, daughter of Steve Clayton, former NASCAR Sprint Cup Series champion and now owner of Pebble Valley Wines in California. Mattie was short for Matilda, a fact he'd dug up on the Internet when he'd first been assigned to the Alan Cargill murder case the winter before. Must have been either a much-loved, or more likely, a very rich relative hanging off a branch of the family tree, to saddle a girl with that name in this day and age, he'd decided as he mentally scrolled through her vital statistics once more: Twenty-eight. Unmarried. Freelance investigative reporter with an impressive number of journalistic credits for someone her age. A childhood spent bouncing back and forth between a playboy father and a mother who had been married more times than your average Hollywood star.

Alan Cargill had been one of the few constants in her life. Lucas was counting on her loyalty to those childhood ties to get him what he wanted today.

"Hello, Mattie," he said coming up on her unawares, catching her staring off into the distance, looking a little wistful. He followed her line of sight. A baby clothes shop seemed to be the object of her attention. Sarah Clayton, her new stepmother, was three months pregnant. He'd read that on a NASCAR blog a week or two earlier. Was Mattie daydreaming of a baby of her own, or merely considering a gift for the new member of her family? He couldn't tell. Despite her ready smile, she wasn't an easy read.

"Oh," she said, jumping in her seat. "You startled me."

"Sorry. I didn't mean to."

"No problem. Have a seat, Detective." She seldom called him by his first name and he hadn't pressed for any lessening of the formality during their infrequent meetings over the winter. Now he wished he had. It would have made it a little easier to broach his plan if they were on a first-name basis. She pushed her sunglasses down on her nose and stared at him over the mirrored lenses. Her eyes, big and wide and the rich brown of a fine mink coat, were her best feature. A guy could get lost in those eyes if he didn't watch himself. She motioned him to take the other seat at the table. "You're late."

He hid a grin. She always had to take the offensive, be the one in control. He didn't mind, if it made her more comfortable. Odds were she wouldn't stay that way for long when he disclosed what he had come to tell her. "I had a conference call to New York. It ran long."

"You could have sent me a text."

He shrugged as he slid onto the seat of the metal chair. It was hot to the touch. The weather in North Carolina took some getting used to. It was the beginning of October and as hot, and even more humid, than mid-August in New York, where he'd been born and raised. "I'm not very good at multitasking. When my boss is chewing my butt, I tend to stay focused on the matter at hand."

"Oh," she said, grudgingly. "That does make a difference." A black-clad waiter with a snow-white towel draped over his arm came from inside the shop to take their order. "Would you like a glass of wine?" she asked. "My treat."

"It's a little early for me."

A quick frown slipped across her expressive face, but remained only a moment. Her smile returned. She had a nice smile. He'd noticed that every time they met. She wasn't a beautiful woman, not by a long shot, but she was very attractive. Her hair was the same dark brown as her eyes, and her mouth was soft and full and looked very kissable. He didn't fool himself, though. Her strong jawline and determined air had been inherited directly from her father, a man with a reputation for getting what he wanted. "Two iced teas," she said. The waiter looked offended but nodded and disappeared inside.

"I can't decide if he's miffed because we didn't order wine, or because we didn't order sweet tea." He hadn't been able to get used to drinking the overly sweet brewed tea that was a Southern favorite.

"I know you don't like sweet tea, Yank," she said.

He lifted an eyebrow. "And you don't like iced tea. Why didn't you order wine? Your father owns a vineyard and winery, doesn't he? Pebble Valley, Sonoma County?" Steve Clayton's vineyard would be sponsoring a NASCAR driver next season. Like the news of his new wife's pregnancy, he had learned of the sponsorship deal from a NASCAR-related Web site.

She tapped the wine list with her finger. She was wearing nail polish, pearly white, just like her lightweight cotton suit and camisole top, all neutral in color and tone. The understated shades were a perfect foil for her hair and eyes. "Dad just released a new Gewürztraminer. It's getting really good reviews. It's basically an aperitif wine, but with enough body and complexity to make it interesting. They carry it here. The offer's still open if you'd like to try it."

"Maybe next time," he demurred. "You know a lot about wine."

She shrugged negligently. "I thought I might go into the family business once upon a time."

"Once upon a time?"

Mattie's mouth tightened into a straight line. She didn't like it when he got personal, he'd learned over the past months. She pushed the wine list away as the waiter returned with two tall, sweating glasses, which he placed on coasters in front of them. When he had marched back into the shop, nose still in the air, she turned to Lucas once more. "Why did you ask to see me, Detective?"

He didn't fall into her trap by asking her to call him Lucas. She would nod, and smile, and go right on referring to him by his title. He gave it to her straight. "The D.A. has decided to drop the murder charges against Armando Mueller," he said. He watched her from behind his own mirrored sunglasses and saw the corners of her mouth tighten, but other than that she showed no outward signs of disappointment. She wasn't just another trust-fund baby amusing herself with a stab at working for a living, he reminded himself, but a successful investigative reporter with an impressive track record. It would take more than this bad news to shake her into revealing her inner feelings, even if the murder victim had been as close as a blood relative to her.

"I figured that would happen once Alan's diamond cuff links turned up at Patsy Grosso's birthday party. You don't have to be Sherlock Holmes to see that blew the case against a New York sneak thief into a million pieces."

"Not to mention the prime suspect being in custody seven hundred miles away," he added.

"Damn. I wanted it to be Mueller, but my gut told me otherwise."

"What did it tell you?" he asked, not discounting her instinct. He used his own often enough.

"That Alan's murder wasn't a random act of violence. Sure, his jewelry is missing but I still think he was killed by someone he knew. Someone he allowed to get close enough to stab him through the heart." Her voice dropped to a whisper. "I loved Alan," she said, raising her eyes to his. He didn't need to see their golden-brown color to know they were swimming in tears. It was his turn to stiffen and draw back slightly. This was way out of character for her. Emotional women gave him the spooks. "He and his wife were always there for me when I was a kid being dragged from race track to race track by my dad." She caught herself, and when she continued her voice was rock solid and hard as cut crystal. "I want whoever killed him to pay for what they did."

"So do I." He leaned forward, elbows on the table. "Get me access to the people who can help solve the murder." He needed to work a deal with Mattie. She was a NASCAR insider. Her father was a past NASCAR Sprint Cup champion. She was Dean and Patsy Grosso's goddaughter. She was part of the NASCAR family.

"You've had access," she responded instantly. "For almost eight months."

"Access, yes. But I'm still an outsider." No one opened up to him, no one relaxed around him, talked about the little things, the small details that might give him a thread of a clue to follow. No one trusted him, and trust was what he needed now to get his dead-in-the-water case back on track. This is where he had to take a leap of faith. Put his trust in a woman he barely knew and didn't much like. "I need to be on the inside," he said. "And I need you to help me get there."

"YOU'RE JOKING, RIGHT?" she asked, leaning back in her chair, putting as much distance between them as she could manage sitting down. He was up to something, but she wasn't sure what it was. Lucas Haines wasn't a man to act on an impulse. There was a reason for everything he did, every move he made. "Do you think anyone will open up to you just because I introduce you to them? You've already interviewed everyone I know, some of them more than once."

"And I've gotten nowhere because I'm a big-city cop with no ties to NASCAR whatsoever."

"That would certainly make me think twice about

telling you anything," she agreed. The corners of his mouth tightened. She imagined his night-blue eyes narrowing behind the mirrored sunglasses, eyes that seemed to bore right through her. She was a little surprised he had admitted his failure quite so readily. But then again, she supposed she shouldn't be. Haines was a straight-arrow, by-the-book cop. He took his responsibilities very seriously and it was completely in character that he didn't shirk the blame when he failed.

"I thought maybe you could help me."

Startled, she laughed out loud. He had nerve; she'd give him that. "Why should I? You've made it more than clear that you didn't need any help from a flighty sports reporter. On more than one occasion, as I recall." She couldn't quite filter all the bitterness out of her voice. She was a damned good investigative reporter. She had to be to nail a top-ten college basketball coach for turning a blind eye to steroid abuse on her team, and to uncover an alumni fund-raising scheme in one of the most prestigious colleges in the Southeast that was funneling tens of thousands of dollars of illegal gifts and services to prospective athletes and their families. But none of that had mattered to the big-city cop.

"I apologize for that." The sun had moved behind one of the iron-fenced trees that shaded the walkway. He took off his sunglasses and twirled them between his lean, strong fingers. His gaze was level and candid. "I'm not always the best team player."

She admired him for admitting that. It was an attribute she shared. She was a lone wolf. She always had been. You couldn't survive the kind of fragmented childhood she had if you relied too heavily on anyone but yourself. "So in other words you're asking me to pull your chestnuts out of the fire for you."

He leaned back in his chair, hooking one arm over the back. "I'm offering you a partnership in solving a crime. My boss has told me in no uncertain terms not to show my face in New York again until I find the real murderer of Alan Cargill."

Mattie grinned, she couldn't help herself. "You've been exiled to Charlotte indefinitely."

"You could say that." He had the grace to look a little sheepish.

"That can't be easy for a big city boy like you, Yank."

"Cut the Yank crap," he retorted. "You spent many of your formative years in California. And even a year in a finishing school in Connecticut."

He'd turned the tables on her again. He knew far more about her than she did him. She had to remember the man was too sharp to toy with. Maybe it was time to call in a favor or two and do some digging into his background. Turnabout was fair play, after all. "It was one semester," she corrected him. "I was, uh, asked to leave after that." That awful episode in her life had occurred during one of her mother's periodic guilt trips for abandoning Mattie to her father's care while she went off to commit serial matrimony. Her mother had begged to have Mattie come live with her. But a sullen sixteen-year-old was not what her mother, pregnant with twins by her fourth husband, had bargained for, and it was off to boarding school with Mattie—but not for long. "I've lived in Charlotte since I was in college. My roots go deep here. There have been Claytons in North Carolina since before the Civil War."

"Wow!" he said sarcastically, then leaned forward,

all business. "I'm asking for your help, Mattie. I need access to NASCAR people. They're a close-knit, close-mouthed bunch, but you're one of them. They'll talk to me if you're around."

She shook her head. "Not necessarily. You're still an outsider. The big-city New York cop. Having me sitting there twiddling my thumbs while you grill my friends won't change anything." She schooled her expression to remain slightly haughty, cool, detached. She'd watched her mother achieve it enough times to make it believable. But inwardly she was humming with nerves. A chance to work with Lucas Haines to solve Alan's murder, a chance to avenge the memory of the man who had always been there for her when she needed him. She couldn't turn him down, no matter what he asked. But he didn't have to know that, not yet.

"If they think you're more than that—"

"Partners in the investigation?" She finished his sentence for him. "Why should they? Nothing's changed. I'm not a cop. Or a CSI, as you've pointed out in the past. I'm just a sports reporter."

"Look…" He ran his hand through his short, dark hair. She was beginning to get under his skin. That pleased her. He was hard to throw off balance. "What if we made it seem as if we were more than working together. What if we let people think we…we were…well…an item."

"What? You mean, a couple? Dating?"

A dark stain spread from his neck to his face. He was blushing. Mattie couldn't believe it. "I know it sounds cliché, but hell, I can't think of any other way to get into these people's confidences and into their heads. Do you want Alan Cargill's murder to be just another cold case that never gets solved, another one where the bad guys win?"

"No."

"Then consider it. All you have to do is be seen with me, take me to a race to get people used to having me around. Level the playing field."

Mattie took off her sunglasses and leaned her forearms on the metal table, clasped her hands around the rapidly warming glass of tea so he couldn't see them trembling. "I won't fawn all over you," she said, making up her mind as she spoke. What choice did she have? She would do a lot more than be seen in company with Lucas Haines to avenge Alan's murder. "That's not my style."

"Mine, either."

"I won't lie to my friends…well, about anything but us dating, that is," she backtracked.

"Agreed, I'm still officially on the case. I'll be up front with everyone I talk to about the murder."

"I have one more condition."

"What's that?" he asked, and she could hear the wariness in his voice.

"I'll smooth the path for you with the people you need to question. I'll pretend we're on a lot better terms than we really are. I'll get you credentialed."

"Credentialed?"

She blew out a puff of air. "You're on my turf now. You won't get far at a NASCAR track without the proper credentials, and I don't mean flashing a NYPD badge in people's faces. I mean, hard cards so you can go anywhere you need to go during a race."

He clenched his jaw, but his tone was gracious enough. "I'd appreciate that."

"And in return I want something from you." She hoped she wasn't the one blushing this time because just saying the words caused images of Lucas Haines doing other things to flash through her head—sensual, sexual things that shocked her thoroughly.

"What?" He stopped twirling the sunglasses and leaned forward.

"I want you to help me search for Gina Grosso."

CHAPTER TWO

LUCAS SAT ON THE EDGE of the bed in his hotel room and looked out the window toward the speedway grandstand visible in the distance. Thunderclouds loomed over it, highlighting the rows of flags snapping in the wind. He glanced at the television screen. The sound was muted but he had it tuned to the weather. Sure enough, a line of thunderstorms was due to move through the Charlotte area later that morning. He hoped it didn't delay their flight. He hated waiting in airports.

"Yeah, Mom, I'm going to California," he repeated patiently, turning away from the TV to focus his attention on his conversation with his mother. "No. I don't know how long I'll be there. Four or five days, possibly longer. I'll try to get back to Brooklyn to see you after that." He listened patiently as Della Haines repeated her usual litany of complaints about him going out of town. She missed him. She had no one to run errands for her. She had no one to be there for her when she needed them. He was just like his father, putting his duty to the police force before his family.

His mother was not a happy woman. She had never been, that he remembered, but since his father's death in the destruction of the World Trade Center on September 11, she had existed in a permanent state of melancholy. She alternated between basking in the reflected glow of her husband's heroic death leading employees of the brokerage firm where he was a security guard to safety, or lamenting her widowhood and her loneliness and lack of proper consideration for her loss.

Lucas loved his mother, but he worked hard at it. His parents' marriage had not been a happy one. His childhood had been filled with tension and long, strained silences. The fault wasn't entirely his mother's. There was enough blame to go around. Marvin Haines had been a taciturn, self-contained man, dedicated to his duty as a police officer. Della was needy and clingy. Lucas often wondered what had caused two such different personalities to believe they were in love. He certainly intended never to make the same mistake as his parents. Marriage was not in the cards for him.

"Mom, I have to go. I'm flying out to Sonoma today. Yeah, that's right, where they have all the wineries." He wondered what she would say if he told her he was going to California wine country to attend a NASCAR race. Or that he was looking forward to it. "Would you like me to bring some back for you? A nice red wine for when we have dinner together next time?" He shoved his foot into the other shoe. His mother was off on a description of all her physical ailments now, and why red wine disagreed with her. He should have known better. "Look, Mom. I have to go. I don't want to miss my flight. Yeah, sure, I'll call when I get out there. Yes, and we'll look into getting the roof shingled, first thing when I get back. I know winter's coming. You take care, Mom. Love you." He flipped the phone shut before she could voice her next grievance.

He bent down to tie his shoes. He wondered if he

should insist she look into the senior apartment complex her oldest sister had moved into the year before. It would be a lot easier on both of them than his trying to keep the three-bedroom rowhouse she had lived in for the past twenty-five years in good repair. He didn't have a nine-to-five job. Sometimes he was on assignment for weeks on end. Months on end, as the Alan Cargill case was turning out to be. He didn't have the time to spare on chores and projects she could well afford to hire a handyman to undertake.

Being an only child made it all the more difficult, but just because he'd always thought it would be great to come from a large family where the duties of caring for an aging and, face it, difficult parent could be divided and shared, it didn't mean he'd ever have one of his own. Not after growing up the way he had, caught in the middle of his parents' enduring but unhappy marriage.

His phone beeped with a text. He didn't even have to look at the display to know it was from Mattie Clayton. She was telling him she was leaving for the airport and making sure he was on his way, too. He didn't respond. He'd had enough of demanding women at the moment.

That wasn't quite fair of him, he decided with a grin. Mattie was demanding but she wasn't a whiner. In all honesty, he'd been surprised she'd agreed so readily to his plan. Then he made himself face up to reality. She hadn't agreed so much as horse-traded him into a deal. She had her own agenda, a search, maybe *quest* would be a better word, that had hit a brick wall of its own. The Gina Grosso kidnapping.

He didn't believe there was any connection between Alan Cargill's murder and the thirty-year-old disappearance of Dean and Patsy Grosso's infant daughter. It didn't make sense. Alan Cargill's past was an open book. He had lived his entire life in the Charlotte area, knew everyone who was anyone in both the business and NASCAR communities, but never once had anyone, including the retired NASCAR Sprint Cup Series champion Dean Grosso and his wife, heard the legendary team owner mention anything about their missing child.

It just didn't compute.

But in exchange for Mattie Clayton opening doors in his investigation of the murder, he was willing to suspend disbelief and give her a hand searching for the whereabouts of Gina Grosso.

He stuck his wallet in his back pocket and clipped his phone on his belt. He'd already placed his gun and ammunition clips in a specially made carrying case. He checked the combination lock and placed the case in his suitcase. He stood silently for a moment debating his decision one last time. He was in possession of all the documentation he needed to carry his service weapon on board the airplane, but he had decided against it, even though it felt like a small betrayal of his father's memory, and the way he and so many others had died that September day.

He locked the suitcase and pocketed the key. He figured his dad would understand. There were protocols to be followed for law enforcement officers carrying weapons onto commercial aircraft. They would call attention to him, and he didn't want Mattie Clayton spooked before they were even off the ground. He had decided discretion was the better option for this trip. There would still be paperwork to fill out, but everything would be far more low-key, less attention grabbing. And he had to admit, regardless of how naked it made him feel to be without his weapon, a four-hour flight in coach would be a lot more comfortable without a shoulder holster under his jacket.

He dropped his key card and a tip for housekeeping onto the dresser, then on a whim unclipped his phone and sent a three-word text to Mattie Clayton:

On my way.

THEY WERE SOMEWHERE OVER New Mexico when she couldn't keep her curiosity to herself any longer. He was impressed she'd lasted that long. "What did the captain want to speak to you about?" she asked, after the flight attendant had trundled past them with lukewarm sodas and tiny packets of pretzels. "I didn't think too much of it on the flight from Charlotte to Dallas, but it happened again when we changed planes. What gives?" He was sitting on the aisle, shoehorned into his seat, but thankfully out from under the bulkhead. He didn't like to admit it, but he was claustrophobic, hated sitting in the window seat. A middle-aged woman reading a book was sitting there. Mattie had drawn the short straw and gotten the middle seat, but she hadn't complained.

"Professional courtesy," he said.

"You're a pilot?" She sounded incredulous.

"No."

"Was it because you're a cop?"

He decided she wasn't going to stop asking until he told her. "I brought a weapon onto his plane."

"A gun?" Her eyes widened. He could see her mind beginning to work. "You're carrying a gun?" She lowered her voice almost to a whisper, evidently not wanting any of the other passengers to overhear their conversation.

"No," he said. "I am not. I checked it with my bag."

"But you told the authorities about it. That's why you filled out those papers at the check-in counter. That's why the pilot wanted to talk to you."

"Regulations," he said. "I have authorization from my commander to carry it on board, but I decided not to."

She studied his profile for a long moment while he fished in the little bag for the last pretzel. "You wanted to, though, didn't you?"

"Most cops aren't comfortable without their weapon," he said, "At least not where I come from."

"That's not the only reason," she said, moistening the tip of her finger and touching it to the salt crystals lying in the bottom of her foil packet. "It's more than that. You've looked like a thundercloud ever since we got to the airport. You don't like being out of control like this, do you?"

He turned his head to face her straight-on. "Don't tell me you're a pop psychologist, too," he said, rolling his eyes.

"No. Well, maybe, a little. I like to find out what makes people tick," she admitted with a grin as she licked the salt off her finger. "That's what makes me good at what I do." He lost his concentration for a moment as her tongue darted out between her strawberry-red lips to lap up the salt. Her hair was pulled up in some kind of fancy clip. It smelled of coconut. Her earrings glittered with the fire of real diamonds. She had pretty ears, small and close to her head, the kind of ears a man liked to trace with the tip of his tongue. Lord, he had to stop letting thoughts like that get a foothold. Fantasies involving Mattie Clayton were strictly off-limits.

"C'mon, fess up," she coaxed. "You're a control freak and not only are you shut up in an aluminum tube seven miles in the air, your gun—the ultimate male symbol of authority—is locked up in the bottom of the airplane. You're on your own if there are any bad guys on board."

The sensual jolt she'd given him dissipated in a rush of annoyance. More than a little of what she'd just said was true. He was rattled enough to tell her the truth. "My dad died in the attack on the World Trade Center. Under the circumstances it goes against the grain to give up my weapon on an airplane."

She blinked but didn't back down. "I'm sorry for your loss," she said and sounded as if she meant it. He felt a little ashamed of himself but brushed it aside. He wasn't just talking to a pretty woman. She was a reporter like the one who had hounded his dad off the Brooklyn precinct where he'd risen to deputy chief after twenty-five years of hard work. He had ended up working security in the doomed towers. "I can see why you don't like feeling out of control this way."

"I don't feel out of control," he snapped, but they both knew he was lying.

"Was…was your father on one of the planes that day?" she asked. There was sympathy in her voice, what sounded like real emotion, but he wasn't fooled. A good reporter, like a good cop, kept their quarry off guard.

"No," he said in a flat voice. Even after all this time it was hard to talk about that day. "He was at work. He was a security guard at a big brokerage firm in the south tower. He led twenty-seven people down the stairs and out to safety. He could have stayed safe himself but he went back to help the other cops he'd worked with for twenty-five years. He never got back out."

"He was a hero," she said very quietly. "You should be proud of him."

He was proud of his father but that didn't make the hurt go away. "He shouldn't even have been there that day," he said. "He and my mom should have been retired in Florida. They would have been if he hadn't been hounded out of his job on the force by a gung-ho reporter bent on finding bad cops wherever she saw a badge."

"She," Mattie repeated, picking up on the pronoun or perhaps the snarl in his voice when he spoke the word.

"Yes, she. Like I said, a gung-ho investigative reporter, idealistic as hell, and bent on cleaning up her little corner of the world."

"Your father got burned in the fallout?"

"He got hounded off the force along with a couple of other good cops. By the time everything got straightened out my dad had given up getting reinstated. He went to work for a security firm in Manhattan and that's why he was in the twin towers that day. It didn't much matter by then that the reporter's sources were found to be feeding her false information. My dad was dead. A visit of condolence from the mayor and the new chief aren't a lot of comfort to a grieving widow."

"And now you have a chip on your shoulder as big as a brick when it comes to my profession. Fair enough," she said. "But just for the record, that's not how I work. I don't get carried away with juicy, too-good-to-be-true info drops from informants. I don't take what anyone says at face value, including New York City police detectives. I do my own research and my own snooping when it's called for. I'm not out to save the world and make myself feel good while I do it. I'm a professional. I can't say I don't like nailing the bad guys, because I do. But I never forget it's my job, not my calling. Understood?"

He should have known she would go on the attack. And surprisingly, he believed what she said. But he wasn't about to admit it to her. He'd already broken enough of his own rules where she was concerned. He couldn't believe he'd shared as much of his dad's story as he had, or let his bitterness for that airheaded reporter get close enough to the surface to seep into his words. Mattie Clayton got under his skin too easily. She pushed all his buttons. He was going to have to be careful around her. Very careful.

THEY HADN'T SPOKEN FOR over two hours. Well, that wasn't precisely true. They'd exchanged stilted pleasantries, polite nothings, but they hadn't had a conversation. Not since he'd laid into her about his father's death, and the bimbo reporter he obviously felt was responsible for it.

The woman certainly had a lot to answer for if what Lucas had told her was true, and even allowing for his bitterness she had no reason to doubt him. There had been a lot of those idealistic and ambitious types in her journalism classes in college. But she wasn't that kind of reporter. She wasn't that kind of woman. Her integrity, her professionalism, meant just as much to her as it did to him, and she intended to let him know that as soon as an opportunity presented itself. She was just waiting for the right moment to bring up the subject again when he beat her to it.

They were loading their luggage into the trunk of a nondescript midsize sedan in the rental car lot at the San Jose Airport before heading toward Sonoma and her father's vineyard. "Look," he said. "I shouldn't have jumped on you like that. What happened to my dad had nothing to do with you."

"You're right. It didn't have anything to do with me," she agreed, taking a quick breath so that she didn't stumble over her words. "But I owe you an apology, too."

"Why?"

"I'm not usually that defensive about my work. It's just that this trip, well, it's making me a little jumpy. I…I haven't been home in a while."

"And you've never mentioned a new boyfriend to your dad, right?"

"Right. Not that it would surprise him. We're not close enough for me to tell him everything that goes on in my life."

"I haven't brought a woman home to meet my mother since the junior prom, so I can see where you're coming from."

That set off a warning bell in her head. There were issues with his mother, as well as his father. Welcome to the club, she thought, thinking of her own complicated relationship with her parents. "But I told you I'm not lying to my friends and family. I plan to tell my father the truth. Do you have a problem with that?"

"Not as long as he keeps it to himself."

"What if my father doesn't want to go along with our scheme?"

"Why shouldn't he? Alan Cargill was his friend, wasn't he?"

"Yes, he was."

"I'd think he'd want to see Alan's killer caught as badly as you do."

"That's right. But at one time or another over the summer you've put a lot of our friends and neighbors under the microscope and given them a hard time."

Only the ones who looked suspicious. "You notice none of them are in custody at the moment," he said, choosing his words with care.

She let that one pass. "And then there's my new stepmother. She's pregnant. I'm not sure she's up to a lot of entertaining."

He raised one eyebrow. "I don't expect to be entertained. Is your stepmother experiencing a difficult pregnancy?"

She felt her face growing warm. "No. I..." Might as well tell him the truth. He was too canny not to figure it out for himself. "I don't know Sarah all that well, yet. It's a little awkward, what with the baby coming and all."

He surprised her by not saying anything more on the subject. "I'll be on my best behavior around both of them."

She managed a smile. She hoped it wasn't as twisted as her insides felt at the moment. The few guys she had brought home to meet her famous father in the last decade had been intimidated as hell by him. Somehow she doubted that would be the case with Lucas Haines. "We won't be seeing much of my dad, anyway," she warned him. "It's harvest season. He spends all his time with the grapes." She loved this time of year, the smells, the anticipation. The sense of urgency to get the grapes off the vine and into the crushing vats at just the right moment, the worry that the weather would not cooperate. Too bad she wasn't going to be able to help out while she was here.

Of course her father wouldn't expect that of her, anyway.

And why should he? She'd pretty much ignored the operation for the last ten years. Why would he expect her to be interested now?

The vineyards were calling her, but before she could listen to that inner summons she had a mission to complete. Finding Alan's murderer came first. Her second mission was almost as important. She was determined to keep looking for Gina Grosso, to reunite her with her family. Exploring the possibility of becoming a winemaker would have to wait.

Mattie held out her hand for the car keys, more in charity with Lucas Haines than she had been in several days. "I'll drive. I know the roads around here better than you do."

Lucas tossed the key ring over the top of the sedan he'd rented without a murmur. Funny, she'd figured him for an SUV type of guy. But then again if his per diem from the police department was as paltry as the ones she got from her editors then she'd have rented a budget car, too. "I was going to suggest that myself," he said, folding his big frame into the passenger seat. "Nothing I like better than a guided tour."

CHAPTER THREE

MATTIE SLOWED THE CAR when they topped the rise above the vineyards. All around them the landscape was green and gold with glints of purple as rich as a royal robe when the sunlight touched a vine still heavy with its burden of fruit. It was October now and the harvest was in full swing. Below them her father's vineyards covered the hillside, row after trellised row, reaching toward the low-slung adobe house and buildings at the crest. Small tractors pulling large containers called gondolas, crawled along the rows while workers filled them with just-harvested grapes.

Lucas whistled softly between his teeth. "Impressive," he said, leaning a little forward in his seat to get a better view. "How long does the harvest take?"

Mattie lifted her shoulder in a shrug. "It depends," she said. "Different varieties of grapes mature at different times. Sugar content is what's important and weather has a lot to do with it. Last year was exceptionally cool and cloudy. The grapes ripened late and harvest stretched into November. My dad was pretty worried. No one staffs for such a late harvest." He looked puzzled. "Grape pickers are skilled workers," she elaborated. "They move from vineyard to vineyard. If the grapes aren't ready to harvest when they're scheduled to move on, you have a real problem."

"That makes sense. Is the harvest on time this year?"

She frowned. "It's on time but barely. There were some late frosts in the valley that did a lot of damage to the vines. It was hit-and-miss, but Dad thinks we're okay." She smiled. His vineyards were one of the few things she and her father could talk about without hitting snags in the conversation.

"Wine making is like any other kind of farming when you come right down to it. Weather is your best friend and your greatest enemy."

She frowned then realized he was teasing her. It surprised her, but she tried not to let it show. "Yeah, I guess you could say that. Too much rain or not enough. Too much sun or not enough. Not quite like raising grain, or cows and chickens and pigs, but at the end of the day weather still rules the show." She put the car into gear and drove down into her father's little valley, turned onto the gravel drive and passed through the big wrought iron gates leading back up the hill to the house and winery.

Rows of trellised vines, already denuded of their fruit, paralleled the road. Mattie rolled down the car window, letting in the warm afternoon breeze, heavy with the mingled scents of grapes and dust and sunshine. The growl of tractor engines and the voices of the harvesters, calling out to one another in a mixture of Spanish and English, carried to them, as well. No one took notice of the car driving by. Time was money for these men and, besides, they were used to traffic on the roadway as tourists and wine aficionados made their way to the tasting room.

She would enjoy showing off the winery to Lucas, she realized. She was proud of what her father had accomplished here. And there would be no more beautiful but transient women in residence to make her feel gauche and unattractive—unwanted. Her father was a married man now.

A father-to-be.

A little shiver of anxiety skittered across her nerve endings. She just couldn't get used to the idea of a baby for her father. Her half sister and brothers were almost grown, but she remembered what it had been like to have a new baby in the family. It had usually resulted in her being pushed out of the nest and sent back to her father. She was too old to be pushed out again, of course, but she still felt strange and lonely and a little lost when she thought about sharing her father's love with a new half brother or sister.

She could see the figures of her father and stepmother sitting at a table on the flagstone patio as she pulled into the private drive that led to the back of the house. "There are my dad and his wife," she said, "They're sort of a bicoastal couple right now. Sarah still teaches motorsports management at Larchmont three days a week. It's a private college not too far from Charlotte," she clarified. "I don't know how much longer she'll keep making the cross-country flight every week, though, what with the baby coming and all." She felt that stab of uncertainty, and maybe even jealousy, again. She was going to have to get a handle on herself. "I'll introduce you. We can get our bags out of the trunk later. Is that all right?"

Lucas nodded without comment. He was wearing the same kind of mirrored sunglasses that most NASCAR drivers preferred, her father included, and she really couldn't decipher a single thing he was thinking. That irritated her enough that she almost forgot how nervous she was about him being with her in the first place.

"Ready?" she said, more to herself than to him.

He removed the sunglasses and hooked them in the neck of his shirt. It was an ordinary dress shirt, snowy white, unbuttoned at the throat. He wasn't wearing a tie and he'd rolled the sleeves up a couple of turns to expose tanned forearms dusted with bronzed hair. His chest hair was darker than the hair on his arms and her eyes lingered there noting the strength in the muscles of his chest where the cotton was stretched thin. "After you," he said politely.

She jerked her gaze upward and caught him smiling at her, a smile that softened the hard angles of his mouth and lightened the shadows in his dark eyes for just a heartbeat, and made her catch her breath a second time in as few minutes. Lucas Haines was a very sexy man.

But she wasn't interested in sexy men at the moment. And particularly not this sexy man, she reminded herself sternly.

"Dad, Sarah. I've brought a friend. I hope you don't mind," she called, waving.

She could feel Lucas tense slightly as he walked beside her toward the stone patio. "You didn't tell them I was coming?"

"I chickened out," she said out of the side of her mouth before she could stop herself, but she recovered quickly. No more thinking about Lucas's sexy chest or Sarah's barely visible baby bump. She was back in control. She'd brought him here for a reason. To find justice for her murdered friend. That was the beginning and end of it. She smiled archly. "Don't worry. The house has five bedrooms. They won't turn you away."

Her father stood up. He was tanned and fit, his blond hair bleached by the California sun. At fifty he didn't have gray hair or an ounce of fat on his lean form. He looked just as he had when he was racing almost twenty years earlier. He always reminded her of Robert Redford in his "Sundance Kid" days. She wouldn't be surprised if Sarah thought the same thing, but she'd never had the nerve to mention the resemblance to her new stepmother. It was just too weird.

"Mattie, you're right on time. No problems on the flight out, I guess." He would have sent his private jet for her if she'd asked, but she hadn't made the request. She wasn't an environmentalist but she couldn't justify the extravagance of two cross-country flights just for her...and Lucas.

Her father came forward and gave her a quick hug then stepped back, smiling. His smiles always warmed Mattie's heart. Today was no exception. She began to relax a little. "Dad, I think you've already met my friend, Lucas. Lucas, my father, Steve Clayton."

"Detective Haines," Steve said, his smile disappearing along with Mattie's peace of mind. "Welcome to Pebble Valley," he said dialing down the charm.

"Thank you. I hope my arriving unannounced this way won't be a problem for you and your wife."

"Of course not," Sarah said, coming forward to stand by her husband. Her stepmother was a dozen years older than Mattie, but didn't look her age. They could easily pass for sisters, Mattie thought. Sarah was a small woman, several inches shorter than Mattie, rounded and feminine with neat brown hair and gray eyes. She smiled with genuine friendliness. "Any friend of Mattie's is welcome here."

"I wasn't aware you and my daughter were so well acquainted, Detective," Steve said.

"We've been spending some time together back in Charlotte," Lucas responded carefully.

Mattie's heart gave a little jerk. She should have told her father she was bringing Lucas with her. It wasn't fair to either of them. It was too late for regrets now. She would have to do the best she could to smooth over the awkward situation.

"Dad, Sarah. Sit down. We have something to tell you," she said, motioning them back to the wrought iron patio table where they'd been sitting. "I should have explained all this to you on the phone, but it's complicated. I thought I could do it better face-to-face." That was true for the most part. What was complicated was the part about her pretending to be dating Lucas Haines.

"All right." Steve put his hand beneath Sarah's elbow and followed his wife back onto the patio. They all took a seat and her father leaned forward in his chair. "What's up, Mattie?"

She glanced at Lucas. "I told you this wouldn't work."

"It's not supposed to work on your father or stepmother, Mattie," he said. "Just on the others."

"What are you talking about?" Steve demanded, his impatience clearly visible.

Better to come right out with it. "I brought Lucas with me so that he could continue his investigation into Alan's murder," she said, feeling tension tighten the muscles of her neck and throat. She always seemed to go about things the wrong way where her father was concerned. What she was doing was a good thing, even if the method she'd chosen was unconventional, but still she felt as if she were in the wrong. "We decided it would be easier to get NASCAR people to talk to him if we appeared to be dating." It sounded as lame now as it had when Lucas had first suggested the ploy. Mortified, she couldn't quite meet her father's steel-blue gaze.

"Dating? Him?" The incredulity in his voice hurt. Mattie winced, unable to help herself.

"Steve." Sarah laid a cautioning hand on his arm.

Her father cleared his throat. "Sorry, Detective. That didn't come out the way I meant it."

"No offense taken. We're aware it's out of character for Mattie to show up at a race with a boyfriend but we were desperate." He gave her a quick sideways glance, a hint of that sexy smile again, as he got back a little of his own. Her father didn't look mollified. He opened his mouth to say something, but Sarah beat him to it.

"I'm confused. I thought they arrested the man that did it. A street thief, I remember reading." Sarah's eyebrows drew together as she concentrated on recalling the particulars of the article. Her stepmother wasn't a beautiful woman, but her features were clear-cut and her eyes were filled with intelligence and a subtle good humor. She looked from Mattie to Lucas and then fixed her assessing gaze on Mattie again. "I gather there have been new developments important enough to warrant this…masquerade?"

"We had to drop the charges against Mueller when Alan's cuff links were found at Patsy Grosso's birthday party. He's still in custody for accepting stolen property, but his lawyer will cop a plea and have him out in a matter of days."

"Someone at Aunt Patsy's party had to have been involved in the murder or they wouldn't have been in possession of the cuff links. Maybe even the murderer himself. I owe it to Uncle Alan to help Lucas find his killer." She sat back in her chair. She had given up reasoning with her stubborn father long ago. She was just as stubborn, she knew that. It was better if they just followed their separate paths. But this time she needed his help. "Please, Dad. We need your cooperation."

Steve glanced at his wife. She gave a slight encouraging nod and Mattie was grateful. "No one will expect you to be best friends with Detective Haines," she said, teasing him a little, which surprised Mattie. She hadn't realized Sarah could be so playful. "You're Mattie's father, after all. You're supposed to be wary of the men she brings home." She shot Lucas a quick smile. "All you have to do is treat him as you would any other guest."

"Guests?" Her father rarely entertained during harvest season. There was just too much that needed his undivided attention during that critical phase of the enterprise.

"We're having a few people over tonight for a little tasting. Mostly NASCAR people." Her father was well known and well respected in NASCAR circles. Sponsor money was hard to come by. Even wealthy owners were always on the lookout for money to fund their teams. They would gladly come west a day early to attend her father's party even though Pebble Valley was several hundred miles north of the Fontana track. "I'm going to be sponsoring a car next year, I told you that didn't I?"

What he didn't say, didn't have to because she already knew, was that the car would have a woman driver. "Who all's coming?"

"Dean and Patsy. Adam Sanford, a couple of other team owners, a couple of the associate sponsors. Some publicity people. A few neighbors and friends sprinkled in so things don't get too intense."

Mattie nodded in agreement about the mix of business and pleasure. "Good strategy."

"I think so, too."

"It's a perfect opportunity for Lucas and me to start our investigations," she said, steering the conversation back to her main purpose.

"I don't like the idea of you targeting our friends this way." Steve looked at them both, his eyes narrowed, his mouth thinned in disapproval.

Mattie found she was holding her breath and let it out on a soundless sigh. She'd disappointed him again, but there was nothing new in that. She leaned forward in her chair. "Dad, they're not your friends if they know anything about Uncle Alan's death that they aren't telling."

She watched him absorb the logic of her words. "All right," he said finally. He still didn't look convinced, Mattie could see that. "Sarah and I will go along with your plan, but I still don't like it."

"Sometimes this job can be a bitch," Lucas said quietly. "Thank you, sir." He held out his hand.

Steve hesitated a moment then returned the handshake. "Don't call me, sir," he said, summoning one of his world-famous smiles. "Call me Steve if you're going to be part of the family."

THE FIRST EVENING HAD GONE well enough, Lucas decided as he stood at the French doors of the room he'd been given and looked out over the moonlit hillside. The harvest was still going on although it was past midnight. Portable floodlights augmented the moonlight, and the small tractors pulling their gondolas full of fruit rumbled through the rows of vines. He had no idea what types of grapes were being gathered, or more than a rudimentary idea of what happened next in the wine-making process. He was even less knowledgeable about the vintner's art than he was about NASCAR.

If you had asked him a week ago what the two had in common, he would have said, nothing at all. Now he knew better. Even in the rarified world of California wine making the potential for marketing to millions of loyal NASCAR fans was sought after.

The gathering this evening had been small. Most of the guests were NASCAR movers and shakers, men and women arriving in their private jets, completely at home as they mingled with a half dozen or so high-powered West Coast business types and a few of Steve's Sonoma friends and neighbors. All very low-key and casual. He had kept himself low-key, as well, showing Mattie enough attention to be in character as her new boyfriend, not enough to make them both uncomfortable. The odd thing was it hadn't been any problem at all to play the part. That surprised him more than a little. Mattie was definitely not his usual type.

A quiet knock sounded on his door. He turned away from the window and went to open it. It was Mattie, wearing an oversize T-shirt and a pair of cotton drawstring pants that clung to her long shapely legs far more provocatively than the manufacturer had intended. "I saw your light shining under the door," she said, "so I knew you were still awake." She had the room across the hall. Probably the one she usually stayed in when she visited her father. Her next words confirmed his supposition.

"Are you comfortable?" She looked around the quietly elegant space with its dark, Spanish-style furnishing, pale gold walls and sheer cream-colored draperies billowing in the soft night breeze. "Sarah was worried the room might not be to your liking. There's more noise from the vineyards on this side of the house, but if she had given you the room next to mine—" she hesitated just a moment "—we would have had to share the same bathroom," she finished in a rush.

"It's fine," he said, meaning it. "I don't often get accommodations like these and I'm enjoying the view, tractor noise and all."

"It is a beautiful house," she said. Her gaze was flickering around the room never quite meeting his, and he realized suddenly she was trying not to look at his chest. He'd forgotten he'd unbuttoned his shirt a few minutes earlier. He'd been absorbed by the moonlit harvest scene outside his window. He'd told her the truth; it was exotic stuff for a city boy like him. He buttoned a couple of buttons and she seemed to settle down a little. "Is there anything you need? Are there enough towels in the bathroom? I forgot to check."

"Plenty."

"Good." She shoved her hands into the slit pockets of her pants and he caught his breath on a jolt of awareness as the gesture pulled the thin cotton tight across her stomach.

He motioned to the armchair near the window. "Want to sit down?"

"No," she said, shaking her head. "I won't keep you

awake any longer. It's been a really long day. It's the middle of the night at home, you know."

"I know." He stepped back and she followed him over the threshold, almost against her will, he thought fancifully.

"I couldn't sleep so I took a walk." She moved toward the window, drawn, as he had been, to the scene beyond. "Dad was checking the crush—that's what we call the harvest out here," she explained. "I went along with him. I love being here this time of year." She looked out the window. "The vintage should be a good one. Not as high a yield as Dad would like, but the sugar content is excellent and the grapes are beautiful. Perfect. They'll make good wine." She changed the subject with her next words. "Did you learn anything talking to Dad's guests tonight?"

He shook his head. "I didn't ask any questions about Alan's death."

"Why not?" She narrowed her eyes. "That's what we're here for."

"The straightforward approach hasn't worked all that well for me so far. Besides, it was a social setting not a police interrogation room. They would have shut me out in a New York minute." He had no more intention of making this conversation into an interrogation than he had his other conversations, earlier in the evening.

She took an exasperated breath and let it out. This time he was the one who had to find another place to look. She had a great figure, feminine and softly rounded in all the right places. He usually liked his women on the skinny side but the longer he was around Mattie the more he appreciated her curves. "I suppose you're right."

"If my usual methods had worked, we wouldn't be standing here right now."

"You don't need to remind me why we're here, or why we're…together." She lifted her chin a little and met his gaze directly for the first time. "I saw you in the corner, talking to Aunt Patsy and Uncle Dean. What was that about?"

"Your godparents were taking their responsibilities toward you seriously, drilling me on how long we'd been seeing each other," he said. "Evidently your bringing a man to this house is quite an unusual happening. I'm not altogether sure they believed me when I said we'd been seeing each other in connection with Alan's murder investigation over the summer and events had taken their natural course."

"I told you it wouldn't work," she said with a little smirk that somehow didn't irritate him as much as it should have.

"I don't think they would have believed we fell head over heels in love at first sight, either." He shouldn't tease her this way. In the first place it wasn't his style and in the second place it was damned unprofessional, but he couldn't seem to help himself. She wasn't wearing any makeup, and he wouldn't have known the difference from the way she looked earlier in the day if he hadn't noticed her eyelashes were several shades lighter, though still thick and curled at the edges. The change made her look about fifteen, far too young for him to be flirting with her, but he failed to heed his own advice. "Patsy told me straight to my face that you weren't my type."

"She's very astute." Mattie wasn't wearing makeup but she was wearing some kind of lip-gloss and her lips were shiny and soft, and her mouth beckoned to be tasted.

He leaned slightly closer. "Dean, on the other hand, reminded her that opposites attract."

She took another step backward and bumped into the chair beside the bed. He reached out and steadied her with his hands on her shoulders and the heady smell of soap and moisturizer and woman filled his nostrils and made him more than a little dizzy and aroused.

"Not in real life," she half whispered.

"I'm not so sure about that." He lowered his head and placed his mouth on hers. For just a moment he felt her lips soften beneath his before she stiffened and backed out of his light grip.

Her eyes were luminous in the glow of the wall sconces on either side of the bed. Enormous, light-filled amber pools, and for a moment they were filled with a desire that matched his own. But only for a moment. She got hold of herself quickly and the now-familiar mulish stubbornness he was coming to recognize as her default emotional setting suffused her face with warmth. "Our bargain is strictly business. Kissing isn't business," she said, with a hiss underlying her words. "Don't do that again."

"It was a real pleasure, though. And good practice in case we have to do it again. We don't want to blow our cover before we even get this investigation started. We're not going to convince anyone we're a couple if you jump like a rattled virgin every time I put my hand on your arm."

"Lucky for both of us I'm not easily rattled or a virgin. Just remember if kissing is called for, I'll pick the right time to do it. We won't blow our cover," she said, turning on her heel in a huff and heading for the door. "I'll see to that."

CHAPTER FOUR

"YOU'RE UP AND ABOUT EARLY this morning." Her father greeted her with a wave of his coffee mug as Mattie joined him on the stone terrace at the rear of the house where he liked to have breakfast on fine mornings. He was wearing jeans and an open-throat shirt, but they fitted him to perfection, and she knew for a fact the shirt was tailor-made.

"I'm still on East Coast time. It's the middle of the morning back in Charlotte," she reminded him. The truth was she hadn't slept all that well. Jet lag—and a stolen kiss—had conspired to keep her awake long into the soft California night. "I walked down to the tasting room gardens and back. The place is looking great. I love the waterfall and gazebo you added since I was here last."

"That was Damon's idea. I forget sometimes how important the physical setting can be to influencing a visitor to buy that extra bottle or case of wine." Damon was Damon Tieri, her father's partner in the winery.

"Marketing is a big part of the business, Dad. You're good at it, too."

"Marketing myself, maybe," he said, turning back to the view over the valley. The fog hanging in the hollows and the sun shining through the already-harvested vines gave the fields the look of hammered gold. "That's all I really had to do until I bought this place. Not quite the same as strapping myself in a race car and driving like hell for five hundred miles, then kissing pretty girls and getting my picture taken."

"Don't underestimate yourself, Dad. You're in a league of your own when it comes to cajoling sponsors into shelling out millions of dollars, massaging team owners' egos and keeping thousands of fans happy and satisfied. The principles are the same," she said, wishing she could tuck her arm through his and give him an encouraging squeeze. But they didn't often show physical affection that way anymore. They hadn't for a long, long time. But maybe they should start doing so again? All she had to do was make the first move.

But what if he thought she was only doing it to get back into his good graces now that a rival for his affection—and her inheritance—would soon make an appearance? Was that what he would think? A niggling fear of rejection paralyzed her movements and before she could banish it, the moment passed.

"Have you had breakfast?" Steve asked.

"Toast and juice. You know Rosita won't let anyone go hungry in this house." Her father's housekeeper was a fabulous cook, and she made it her business to see no one left Pebble Valley without gaining a pound or two. It was a point of honor.

"Patsy and Dean left before dawn to fly down to the track, and I haven't seen Lucas, but Sarah's on her way down. Why don't you join us for breakfast? Some fruit and coffee, at least. It's going to be a long day. We'll be flying down to the track, getting settled in the condo, might be a very late lunch. Sure you don't need something to boost your constitution?"

Mattie forced a grin. "No. Don't tempt me. I never eat breakfast, you know that."

His smile vanished. "There are a lot of things I don't know about you anymore, Mattie."

She held her tongue. There were a lot of things he'd never known about her. But those days of resenting him for his jet-setting lifestyle, when she'd stayed behind with an ever-changing series of nannies, were past. "You two go ahead. I'd better see what's become of Lucas. Maybe he overslept."

"Somehow I find that hard to believe," Steve said, crossing his arms over his chest as he surveyed the ongoing harvest work with a critical eye.

"Yeah, me, too. He's probably been out jogging up and down the hill at least twice." She was only half joking. That kind of exercise routine would be exactly what she'd expect of the man.

Steve must have picked up on the sharpness in her voice. He turned to give her his full attention. "Are you sure you're doing the right thing with this fake romance business? These are our friends, Mattie, and my business acquaintances, you're attempting to deceive."

Mattie felt herself stiffen. She couldn't help it. Dean and Patsy, all the Grossos. Alan's son, Nathan, who had briefly come under suspicion himself, earlier in the year. They were all friends. She didn't want to see their actions called into question. They wanted to know the truth about Alan's death, too. Didn't her dad know it went against the grain to be less than honest with them? He should know without having to be told that it made her uncomfortable to be part of such a scheme, but it was the only way she could contribute to finding Alan's murderer. She had disappointed her father again, she could tell by the look on his face. That was nothing new. They had been disappointing each other for years.

"They're my friends, too, Dad," she said slowly and carefully. "I don't like deceiving them any more than you do. But ever since Alan's cuff links were found at Aunt Patsy's birthday party it seems more and more likely that whoever killed him, or at least someone closely connected to the murder, has as much access to NASCAR as you or I do."

"I know," he said, letting out his breath in a soundless whistle. "It's hard to believe it could be someone we know, maybe even someone we care about, but it's becoming more and more obvious that it is. That's why Sarah and I won't blow your cover. But if this scheme backfires—"

"It won't, Dad. I promise." She wanted to ask him what, exactly, he meant by that cryptic remark. That her NASCAR friends would shun her if they learned she was, in effect, spying on them? Or that she needed to watch her step, and her heart, around Lucas? Her lips tingled with the memory of last night's kiss and she wondered if it was the latter warning her father meant to convey. Before she could gather her courage and ask, they were interrupted.

"Here you are," Sarah said, coming around the corner of the house, Lucas at her side. He didn't look as if he'd only had four hours sleep in the last twenty-four, Mattie thought resentfully. His dark hair glistened in the hazy morning sunlight, still damp from a recent shower. He, too, was wearing an open-collared shirt and jeans, and though his hadn't come from an exclusive Beverly

Hills tailor, he looked just as handsome—dangerously handsome—as her father. "I found Lucas wandering around the house, looking lost and hungry."

"I wasn't lost," he said. "I was heading straight for the kitchen."

Sarah smiled up at him. "Then we need to get you fed." She was wearing a loose blouse in a light gauzy fabric and a pair of cropped pants in shades of green and cream. Maybe it wasn't a good color for her; she looked a little pale, a little drawn.

"Mattie's already eaten," Steve announced. "But I'm sure she'll join us for a cup of Rosita's coffee."

Sarah turned a bit paler, if that was possible. "You three go ahead. I'll join you in a couple of minutes."

"Are you all right?" Mattie's father stepped forward quickly, laid his hand on Sarah's arm.

"I'm fine," she said. "Or I'll be fine soon enough. It's just—" She waved her hand in apology and hurried inside through the open French doors.

"Morning sickness," Steve said, looking a little grim. "Sarah's been having a lot of trouble with it." He looked torn, as if he couldn't decide whether to stay with Mattie and Lucas or follow his wife into the house.

"Go ahead, Dad," Mattie said. Her first official act as big-sister-to-be: send her father after his ailing wife. "I'll see that Lucas gets some breakfast. Go to Sarah."

Steve looked relieved and Mattie was glad she'd made the offer. "Thanks, Mattie. She's, well, she'd never want me to say this, but you know she's over forty. Everything's going great with the baby, but her age puts her in a higher risk bracket. I…I'm kind of worried about her."

She hadn't thought of that. Lots of women over forty

had babies these days, but still, as her father had just said, her new stepmother was definitely in a higher risk category. Mattie wondered if she should offer to go inside with her dad to see if Sarah was okay, then pictured herself standing awkwardly outside the bathroom door while Sarah was sick on the other side and decided against it. Not now. Not yet. It was too soon to become that close a friend to Sarah.

"I WOULDN'T HAVE BELIEVED IT if I wasn't seeing it with my own eyes," Sophia Grosso Murphy said, pointing her goblet of Pebble Valley Syrah in Mattie's direction. "You, Miss-never-get-serious-enough-about-a-guy-to-bring-him-home-to-meet-the-folks, brought a guy all the way to California to meet the folks. It's a miracle."

Sophia, Mattie's friend for almost half her life, was a bit tipsy. She wasn't much of a drinker and she was on her second glass of wine. Mattie couldn't blame her friend for celebrating a little. The Syrah was excellent and Sophia's husband, Justin Murphy, had just won the pole for Sunday's race. He was still in the running for the championship but not as high in the points standing as Mattie knew he wanted to be. The pole position was a boost to his ego, and to Sophia's. Mattie plucked the endangered wineglass from Sophia's hands and set it on the table. "It's a tasting, Sophia," Mattie said with a grin. "Not a chugalug contest."

They were gathered in one of the luxury boxes at Fontana, a track in Southern California where one of the Chase for the NASCAR Sprint Cup races was held each October. The four of them had flown down in Steve's jet the day before and were staying in a town house at a private golf course a couple of rail stops from the racetrack. Mattie always smiled to herself when she thought about arriving at a NASCAR race in a train. It didn't seem right somehow, but lots of things about racing in California were different from other venues. Track food here included gourmet offerings from celebrity chefs and wine tastings, such as the one they were attending now in one of the track's skyboxes. The food was different, the climate was different. The fans were different, too. Hollywood movers and shakers and tanned and toned Angelenos and Beverly Hills millionaires joined the crowds. But the racing was the same, and that's what counted.

Sophia grinned and shook her finger at Mattie. "Don't go lecturing me. I'm not tipsy. Just happy." She looked over Mattie's shoulder and her smile turned incandescent. Mattie didn't even have to turn around to know that Justin had just entered the room. Her friend was head over heels in love with her new husband, and it didn't take a crack investigative reporter to figure that out.

Sophia lifted her hand in a little wave. "Over here," she mouthed. Mattie scooted around in her chair to wiggle her fingers in the handsome driver's direction. "He looks pleased with himself." Mattie grinned at her friend.

"If he drives Sunday like he did today, he's got a good chance of winning the race. He always drives well here."

Justin was still in his orange-and-brown Turn-Rite Tools uniform. He probably had sponsor obligations later in the afternoon. Mattie knew her deduction was accurate when he took a bottle of springwater from a hovering waiter instead of a glass of wine or a beer as he ambled over to them.

"Hi, Mattie," he said, shooting her a grin as he leaned

over Sophia's shoulder to give her a quick kiss just below her ear. Sophia shivered a little and tilted her head to rub her cheek against his. Mattie shivered a little, too, picking up on the sensual undercurrents that ran between the newlyweds. She didn't usually let that kind of affectionate display unnerve her, but for some reason today it did. It was probably from being around her father and his bride. Love was in the air. It had nothing whatsoever to do with that dare-you-to-retaliate kiss Lucas had blindsided her with the first night of their stay in Pebble Valley.

Nothing at all.

"Hi, Justin," she said as he took a seat next to Sophia. "Congrats on taking the pole today."

"Thanks. The car was sweet right off the hauler."

"Track conditions are supposed to be the same tomorrow."

He gave her one of his patented lady-killer grins. "I sure as heck hope so. Winning here will put me just about even in the points race with my esteemed brother-in-law. With four races left to go—" he shrugged broad shoulders "—well, anything can happen."

"And probably will," Sophia said, smiling.

"Since your father-in-law isn't defending his title, either you or Kent could lay claim to be the heir apparent," Mattie teased gently. The Grossos and Murphys had feuded for nearly half a century, but Justin and Sophia daring to fall in love the year before had helped reconcile the two NASCAR dynasties.

"Garrett Clark might have something to say about that," Justin admitted grudgingly. "He's been driving the wheels off his car the last couple of races. It's going to take more than sitting on the pole this week to overcome his lead."

"If anyone can do it, you can," Sophia said, her eyes shining with pride. "You're a natural. Everyone says so."

Justin frowned a little as he took a long swallow of his bottled water. "Just having a feel for the car isn't always enough these days," he said, half to them, half to himself. "It's a high-tech world out there, and us seat-of-the-pants guys are becoming an endangered species."

"That's what you need me for, to pull you kicking and screaming into the new millennium," Sophia said, laughing. "Mattie, here comes your beau."

"He's not my—" Mattie almost gave herself away. She hadn't had a chance to be private with Sophia since they arrived at the race track, and the skybox was way too public for her to go into the details of her pact with the devil. She would have to play her part in their charade even with her friends, and the deception spoiled her enjoyment.

"Hello," Lucas said, nodding cordially as he walked up beside Mattie's chair. He was holding a glass of red wine in his hand. The same one he'd been carrying for the past half hour, Mattie realized. He might look relaxed and at ease, but beneath the surface he was all business—a cop, thorough and ruthless when he needed to be. She shivered again but this time the sensation was not as pleasurable as it had been before.

"Sit down, Lucas," she said more sharply than she had intended because her guilty conscience was still pricking her. "You're giving me a crick in my neck."

"Sorry," he said affably, sliding onto a vacant chair and hitching it several inches closer to Mattie's than it needed to be. "Mattie must have gotten up on the wrong side of the bed this morning."

Sophia's eyes widened. Mattie shot Lucas a smoldering look. "I slept very well," she said repressively. "I always do."

"That's good to know."

"How is your investigation going?" Justin asked. He had met Lucas a time or two over the summer, Mattie knew, and didn't seem intimidated by him. Of course, Mattie doubted Justin would be intimidated by anyone, except maybe Sophia's ninety-three-year-old great-grandfather Milo, patriarch of the Grosso clan and NASCAR legend.

"I'm hoping it will go better now that Mattie and I have teamed up," Lucas said, giving her a smile that she would have sworn was genuine if she hadn't caught a quick glimpse of swiftly concealed irritation behind his eyes.

"You could have knocked me over with a feather when Mom and Dad told me you were dating," Sophia said. "I know Mattie and I haven't been keeping in touch as much as we used to, but I never thought… I mean, you two…" She colored prettily and threw up her hands. "You're just so—"

"Completely unsuited to each other?" Mattie asked, batting her eyelashes as Lucas tightened his grip on his wineglass.

"No. No, of course I didn't mean that," Sophia hurried to explain. "But, well—oh, I don't know what I mean."

"Opposites attract." Mattie forced herself to lean closer to Lucas's shoulder as he put his hand over hers on the table.

"Like a magnet and iron filings." Sophia clapped her hands together, almost spilling her wine.

Justin rescued the wineglass with an indulgent smile for his bride. "Talk about opposites attracting. With all the family baggage we had weighing us down, it's a wonder we ever made it down the aisle."

"But we did," Sophia said, settling back in her chair, her hand on Justin's arm. "And we are going to stay married for a long, long time."

"I'll drink to that," Justin said, and lifted his bottle of springwater.

"Me, too," Mattie seconded. Justin and Sophia had gone though a lot to be together. Their love was the real thing. For a moment she felt a pang of pure, unadulterated envy. She wanted that kind of romance, that kind of love, but she was afraid she'd never find it.

"I've got to head over to the Turn-Rite hospitality tent," Justin said, glancing at his watch. "Would you like to come with me?" he asked Lucas, pointing his water bottle in the direction of the laminated plastic card hanging from a lanyard around Lucas's neck. "You have your hard card. We could stop by the garage and the hauler, take a look at the car."

"Thanks," Lucas said with a grin, a real smile, disarming and charming as hell. "I'd like that." The smile altered slightly and became icy and dangerous, at least to Mattie's way of thinking. "If it's okay with Mattie. Mind if I take off with Justin for a couple of hours?"

"Of course not," she said. "But don't forget we're having dinner with Dad and Sarah tonight." She shifted her gaze to Sophia. For some reason she was having trouble matching look for look with Lucas. "Dad wants Lucas to meet his partner in the winery. Damon's flying in for the race tomorrow."

"I wouldn't miss it for the world," Lucas said silkily. He bent forward just slightly at the waist and Mattie leaned back in her seat to forestall him kissing her.

Without missing a beat, he held out his hand to Sophia instead. “Nice seeing you again.”

“You, too, Lucas.”

Justin leaned over and gave her a peck on the cheek. “See you back at the motor home.”

“I’m making lasagna. Don’t eat too many snacks at the hospitality suite.”

“Nana’s recipe?”

“Who else’s?” Sophia’s great-grandmother Juliana’s cooking was renowned throughout NASCAR.

“I promise you not a bite of food will pass my lips.”

She laughed. “Lucas, will you see he keeps his word?”

“I will,” he said with a laugh, but it sounded to Mattie as if he meant it.

They watched the two men walk away.

“I didn’t mean to embarrass you earlier,” Sophia apologized. “Sometimes my tongue gets away from me.”

“We are an odd couple, aren’t we?” Mattie longed once more to tell her friend the truth, but there were too many people in the small space who might overhear.

“Is Lucas going to be in Charlotte for the race next week?” Sophia asked. “I want him to meet Nana. I think he’s interviewed everyone who has any connection to NASCAR but her.”

“She didn’t go to New York last winter, did she?” Mattie recalled.

“No. It was only a couple of weeks after she had her gallbladder removed and the doctor didn’t want her to travel. Granddad did, though. Lucas interviewed him, but he had nothing to offer. He and Kent left the ballroom early, before…before Alan was murdered.” Sophia stared down into her wineglass before meeting

Mattie's gaze once more. "Do you think they'll ever find who did it?"

"We will if I have anything to say about it."

Sophia laughed. "Oh, Mattie. You haven't changed a bit. Always so adamant. Always determined to set the world straight." She looked thoughtful for a moment then gave Mattie a knowing smile. "Maybe you and Lucas aren't such opposites after all."

CHAPTER FIVE

LUCAS LEANED BACK in the plush leather seat and took a long swallow of his beer. The glass he was drinking from was lead crystal, the beer icy cold. They'd had prime rib for dinner and some kind of champagne trifle for dessert, and no one could have guessed that the medium-rare beef or the deceptively simple dessert had been prepared in the galley of a private jet thirty-five thousand feet in the air. He had to admit he could get used to the lifestyle he'd been living the last seventy-two hours without much trouble at all.

Mattie was sitting next to him, immersed in her own thoughts, tapping away on the keyboard of her laptop as she had been for the last forty-five minutes or so. She was wearing a Shelly Green No. 411 cap with the brim pulled down to shield her eyes from the glare of the overhead cabin lights. From what he'd seen of Shelly's driving on Saturday, he figured Steve had made a good choice for the winery's sponsorship.

Mattie pushed back the brim of the ball cap and squinted down at the screen, then tapped the enter key to save her work. The cap should have looked silly on a grown woman, but somehow it didn't. It looked damned sexy. He shifted uncomfortably in his seat.

They were alone at the front of the plane. Mattie's

father and stepmother were sitting in the rear of the cabin with Tieri. The trio was immersed in details of their upcoming NASCAR sponsorship. Lucas had to admit he wouldn't mind being privy to the conversation. The intricacies of the business side of NASCAR were as interesting as the races themselves—he smiled to himself. Well, almost as interesting.

He'd played basketball in high school, pickup hockey in the winter. He enjoyed professional football and always tried to catch a couple of Yankees games when he could. Stock car racing had always been just at the edge of his sports consciousness, like bobsledding during the winter Olympics, or watching professional bowling on TV.

But over the summer that had changed. Now he was hooked. He'd been to a couple of tracks over the season in connection with the murder investigation but never behind the scenes, never part of the show the way he'd been this weekend. He'd had trouble, sometimes, keeping his mind focused on his real purpose with the maelstrom of color and motion and noise—ear-shattering, chest-thumping noise, the sheer volume of which he'd never encountered before. And the speed—the blur of cars streaking past faster than the eye could follow, here one instant, far down the track the next. He couldn't imagine trying to control a ton and a half of sheet metal and fiberglass wrapped around a 850-horsepower V-8 engine, being propelled around a high-banked oval at close to two hundred miles an hour, but if he ever had the chance to find out he'd jump on the opportunity so fast it would make Mattie's head spin.

"You look pleased with yourself," Mattie said above the muted roar of the engines. It was late in the evening, the middle of the night back in North Carolina. Good thing jet lag had never been a problem for him.

"It was a good weekend," he said.

"From a standpoint of fantastic food, excellent wine and seats on the Start/Finish line for the race?" she asked, raising her eyebrows a fraction of an inch. She had nice eyebrows, he decided. Just enough of an arch to give her a sultry, come-hither look that drew a man's attention.

"Not to mention a tour of the Turn-Rite garage and hauler and access to Victory Lane after Justin won the race," he returned, knowing better than to let her get the upper hand so early in the conversation.

"I'm glad you had a good time," she said, closing the lid of her laptop with a snap. "But what about Alan's murder? Come up with anything there?"

He shook his head. "No," he replied. There was no use lying to her, or even skirting the truth. She was far too sharp for that. "I was earning trust this weekend, not making people more suspicious of my motives than they already are."

"I didn't expect you to find a murderer lurking in my father's skybox or the Grossos' motor home. But I did think you'd have made some observations, maybe drawn a useful conclusion or two."

"Nobody confessed to me on pit road or confided that they knew who the murderer was while we were in line at the concession stand, if that's what you're asking."

She frowned, not liking his answer. "It's going to take more than one race to make you acceptable to NASCAR people," she pointed out.

"Precisely why I said 'yes' when Sophia Murphy invited us to join them for one of her great-grandmother's dinners before next week's race." The race was at the Charlotte speedway on Sunday, home for most of the drivers and their teams. Even he, the outsider, sensed the anticipation of drivers and team members alike to return to stock car racing's home turf. "Juliana's anxious to meet the man who was able to snag 'Our Mattie.'"

"Sophia said what?" Mattie sat up straighter, swiveling her chair to get a better angle. "Snag me?"

"Evidently you have a reputation for being skittish about relationships."

Mattie's eyes narrowed to golden-brown slits. "She wouldn't dare say that about me to you, of all people."

"Maybe not in those exact words, but she did give me some pointers on handling you."

"Handling me? She will pay," Mattie decreed, but he could tell she wasn't serious.

"She cares about you." He knew the change of tactics would throw her off guard, and it did.

"Well…I care about her, too. And I'm going to tell her the truth about us as soon as I have a chance."

"Don't," he said. "Please." He was learning when to back off with her and now was one of those times. "I like Sophia and Justin, but she doesn't strike me as someone who has a lot of patience with subterfuge. None of the Grossos do. If they shut me out, we're back to square one."

"As far as I can tell we haven't moved off square one all weekend." She opened her laptop and placed the screen so they could both see it.

"What's that?" he asked, leaning forward to bring the image into view.

"It's a time line for Alan's murder, as well as what's happened since. I'd appreciate it if you'd fill in some of the blanks for me. So far this partnership seems to be going all in one direction. Yours," she said pointedly. "Not only have you not told me if you have a suspect in mind, you haven't even admitted to a hunch, an inkling of who the murderer is."

"I don't work on hunches," he said. "And if I did, I'm not sure I'd be ready to tell you."

She stiffened, "Why not?"

"Because I can't be sure you wouldn't take off and make a citizen's arrest, blow the whole case out of the water."

"You really are a jerk," Mattie shot back. "You don't win a regional Pulitzer for investigative reporting by being unprofessional, untrustworthy or running your mouth to whoever stops to listen."

"I stand corrected." He wasn't relaxed anymore. He'd touched a nerve with his last unguarded comment. He would have to do some damage control.

"Don't play me, Lucas," Mattie said, gritting her teeth. "I've been played too many times in the past. I've been able to see through a smoke screen since I was a little girl. Let's get this straight once and for all. I'm as much a professional as you are."

A Pulitzer Prize. He hadn't known that about her. Not that it made any difference. He'd already decided she was one smart lady. "I'm not playing you, Mattie," he lied. He had been playing her—to a point. He hadn't intended to make this a real partnership no matter what he told her, and she was beginning to see through his scheme.

She snorted. "What do you call it then?"

The question had a hard edge that demanded an answer. What was he doing? He enjoyed her company and the access she gave him to the inner circle of NASCAR but was he willing to take her into his confidence? Turn this charade into a real working partnership? It wasn't his style. It wasn't the way he worked. From the closed, set look on her face, he figured she'd caught the drift of his thoughts. "Mattie—"

"No more deals," she interrupted. "I'll lay my cards on the table if you'll do the same. Otherwise all bets are off. We're going to come to a parting of the ways." Her mouth set in a tight line. "You'll be just one more of Mattie's unhappy love affairs for everyone to shake their heads over behind my back. So sad but so typical, they'll say. All I have to do is drop a word here and there about what a jerk you are—believe me, right now I could win an Oscar for my performance. You'll be back out in the cold, Detective Haines, and have no doubt, I'll make sure no one tells you anything more than name, rank and serial number. Do I make myself clear?"

Lucas knew he'd made a monumental mistake. He'd insulted both her pride and her professional judgment. He needed to backtrack big-time to make things right, give in to her demands to be better informed on the details of the case. He went through his evidence file in his head, what little there was of it. His notes on his interviews with her family and friends. She might have some insights on those that would help him down the road, some observation or personal anecdote that he'd missed. The information on the street thief, Armando Mueller? Why not? Maybe there was some nugget of information buried in the lengthy file that he'd overlooked. It had happened before to better cops than him.

The autopsy report? She would probably insist on seeing it. The crime scene photos? Possibly, but he would do his best to talk her out of it. Why inflict that trauma on her? He already realized how deep a personal blow Alan's death had been to her. New tactics. A new direction, with, hopefully, a new resolution.

Starting now.

"I apologize, Mattie. I didn't mean to insult you."

She gave him a stiff nod. "Accepted. But I still think this whole idea of us pretending to be a couple isn't working."

"It's too late. We're committed. We need to go through with it, at least until after the Charlotte race. Look, Mattie. You're right. I admit that. We need to quit running on parallel tracks if we're going to make any progress on Alan's murder case."

"Or Gina's kidnapping?"

"There is no link between the kidnapping and Alan's murder," he said. He'd determined that last summer. There was just no connecting thread to the thirty-year-old kidnapping and the more recent crime. Not that he could see, anyway.

"I'm not so sure," she said, her lips set in a stubborn line. For the first time he noticed signs of strain and fatigue at the corners of her mouth and eyes. He could feel his own exhaustion beginning to catch up with him.

"Your stepmother's looking this way. Don't pull away." She tensed but did as he asked. Her fingers were narrow and slim, her skin soft beneath his calloused palm. He felt a jolt of low-voltage electricity skitter across his nerve endings and for a split second he remembered the taste and feel of her mouth on his when he kissed her. He forced his mind back to the present and the hurt and angry woman facing him. God, he wasn't good at this man-woman, give-and-take thing. He'd never had a good role model, he guessed. His parents' lives together had been more of an armed truce than a marriage. But he had to try to maintain a working relationship with Mattie.

"Let's give it a rest for tonight, get some sleep, start fresh—" he glanced at his watch "—later today. What do you say I pick you up around six this evening and take you to dinner? I'll lay all my cards on the table and you can tell me what you make of the whole damned, complicated mess. You're right. I'm not a good team player, but I'll do my best to be one this time."

"We both need to improve our teamwork," she admitted, relaxing a little. "It's a deal," she said, swiveling her seat to greet Sarah and the other two men as they made their way forward, but she kept her brown eyes firmly fixed on his. "But let's do this at my place. We're liable to run into just about anyone you can name in NASCAR on a Monday night in Charlotte or Mooresville."

"You cook?"

"I'm as good a chef as Grace Winters when it comes to ordering takeout," she said with a tiny, wicked smile hovering at the corner of her mouth. "And besides, if we eat at my place, I won't have to be nice to you in public."

CHAPTER SIX

SHE'D MADE A MISTAKE inviting him to her apartment; she was certain of it now that it was too late to change her mind. She hadn't entertained a man here for, well, never. She'd moved in just after her last almost-serious romance hit the skids and she hadn't cared enough about any guy since to bring them here.

Maybe because she didn't much like the place herself? It wasn't bad as apartments went on the second floor of a three-story town house. She had one bedroom, a separate galley kitchen, a small balcony looking down on the same stretch of trendy shops and restaurants where she'd met Lucas the week before. But it wasn't a home. Far from it. It was just a place to keep her things between assignments. The decorating was strictly landlord-neutral in shades of cream and brown. She hadn't even hung any pictures on the walls. She'd meant to, really, but somehow she'd never gotten around to it.

At least he would be comfortable. Her furniture was good quality because her mother had gone with her to pick it out during one of Karen's sporadic attempts at mother-daughter bonding, but it was too formal and grandiose for the small living area. Once Mattie had added the flat-screen TV and the entertainment center that held it, there was scarcely room to turn around without bumping into something. She really needed to rethink the space.

It was too late to change anything now. He would be here any moment. It was clean, at least, and she'd put fresh towels in the bathroom in case Lucas went in there. As for her bedroom. She had just turned her back and closed the door. He definitely wouldn't be going in there. This wasn't a date. It was a working meeting, a strategy session, nothing more. She was feeding the man, yes, but that would be as far as it went.

The doorbell rang and she went to answer it. He was punctual; she'd give him that. She took a quick breath to steady her heart rate, annoyed with the quick, unwelcome uptick in her pulse she couldn't seem to control.

"You found the place," she said, stretching her mouth into a smile. Lord, he looked good, and smelled even better. The day's growth of beard that darkened his lean jaw didn't hurt the image, either. Mattie frowned. He didn't look as if he'd gotten less than four hours sleep—the amount she'd managed after the all-night flight from the West Coast. He was dressed in jeans that looked worn and comfortable and a pale green shirt beneath a black leather jacket darkened on the shoulders by the light rain falling outside.

He was carrying a bottle of wine and a briefcase in one hand, and a bouquet of flowers in the other, spider mums in shades of orange and amber and purple and feathery grasses that made her think of fall. "These are for you," he said, handing over the flowers.

"Thank you," she managed without stuttering. "They're very nice." It was a courteous, old-fashioned gesture, and her pulse picked up a little more speed.

"And the wine," he said. "I know it's redundant bringing wine to a winemaker's daughter but my mother taught me to always bring a nice bottle when you've been invited to share a meal."

Share a meal, a common phrase, but it sent a nervous shiver of pure sensual awareness up and down her spine. They would be sharing a meal, alone, for the first time.

"It's one of my dad's," she said, and this time she didn't have to work to form a smile. "Thank you. Where did you find it?"

"At that shop where we met last week," he said as he stepped over the threshold, immediately reducing the breathable air in her small apartment. "I stopped on my way here. The clerk recommended it. Says he is building a sizable clientele around your dad's label. I thought you'd like to know that."

"I'll tell him the first chance I get. Let me take your jacket."

"I'll get it," he said, handing her the wine bottle. He shrugged out of his coat and hung it on one of the hooks beside the door. He set the briefcase on the floor beneath it and followed her out of the tiny foyer into the main room.

"That's where I got the flowers, too. It's a nice street of shops, kind of reminds me of some of the neighborhoods in Brooklyn where I grew up."

Mattie wrinkled her forehead. "I've never been to Brooklyn," she said. "I guess I've always had the impression that it's gritty and gray, work-worn, you know, like in old black-and-white movies."

"There are places like that, but there are also a lot of nice neighborhoods to raise a family. Less expensive than living in Manhattan. I should know."

"You live in Manhattan. My mom and her new husband have a place there."

"The Upper East Side?"

"Central Park West."

He whistled. "Way out of my league. I like your street, though."

"This is a nice neighborhood," Mattie agreed, taking the flowers to the kitchen. "Not that I spend a lot of time here. I travel a lot." She hoped she could find her one-and-only good vase in the crowded cupboards and didn't have to resort to sticking them in a martini shaker.

She did find the vase, after a short search, complete with crystal marbles in the bottom so that she could actually make the flowers into some sort of arrangement. "There," she said, setting the finished product on the pass-through that connected the kitchen to the living room. "They're lovely, like autumn in a mountain meadow. Thank you, again."

Lucas had taken a seat on one of the stools on the living room side as she worked. "Seeing mums everywhere reminds me that summer is really over. Back home, the trees are turning and the kids are getting ready for Halloween."

"Lots of Halloween decorations are out here, too." She took two glasses from the cupboard and polished them on a towel. She set one on the counter in front of him then dealt with the wine. He didn't offer to do the task for her and she liked that. He was obviously a man confident enough in his own masculinity to let a woman tackle a wine cork on her own. Of course the state-of-the-art wine opener her father had given her a couple of Christmases ago made easy work of even the most stubborn corks. "Seems to start earlier and earlier every year," she observed, pouring the ruby liquid into both their glasses.

"You've noticed that, too?"

"Yeah, and then they seem to skip right over Thanksgiving and go to Christmas."

He grinned. "You sound like my mom."

"Oh, dear," she answered not certain how to take that remark.

He flushed and she found it oddly endearing. Lucas was one of the most restrained men she knew. It gave her a jolt of feminine power to realize she could rattle him, if only slightly and only for a moment or two.

"I meant that in a good way. My mom's not a happy woman but she has her good points." He seemed to choose his words carefully. "She loves holidays. She hates to see any of them slighted, especially the family ones, like Thanksgiving."

"I agree with her there," Mattie said, although many of her own Thanksgivings had been spent not with her parents, but with school friends and her father's cousins, while Steve escorted a supermodel or starlet to some high-profile destination or another, and her mother concentrated on impressing yet another new set of in-laws. When she was a teenager, Mattie had even spent one or two Thanksgivings with Sophia and her family. Those were the ones she remembered best. The food: incredible amounts of it filling Juliana's big kitchen with wonderful smells; laughter; the conversations that ranged from politics to movie reviews to sports and art but always returned in the end to the subject dearest to their hearts—NASCAR.

She realized Thanksgiving would be coming up soon and she didn't know where she would be on that most family-oriented of days. Her father and Sarah were a unit now, and perhaps Sarah would want them to spend the holiday with her family? Mattie didn't know her mother's plans yet, but she doubted they would include her. Even thinking about spending the day alone depressed her. "Let's eat," she said, changing the subject. "Are you tired of barbecue?"

"No," he said emphatically. "Most definitely not."

She laughed. "One thing I know is that most men never get tired of eating charred meat."

"It's hardwired into our DNA."

"A caveman ancestral memory, I suppose. I brought some for you to try from a really good place I know of way out in the country. It's called Mikey's, ever heard of it?"

"Can't say that I have, but I haven't spent much time down here exploring the countryside."

"Mikey's is famous for its barbecue and banana pudding. I've got some of both," she said, opening the refrigerator to pull out the foam containers she'd gotten earlier in the afternoon. She warmed the meat in the microwave while she filled two plates with sides of baked beans and coleslaw and took silverware and napkins out of the drawer. They didn't talk much as they ate, but Mattie didn't find the silence uncomfortable. Lucas was obviously not one for idle chitchat and neither was she.

They took their wineglasses with them when they left the table. Lucas fetched the briefcase and sat down beside her on the couch. The street outside was quiet and she could hear the patter of raindrops on her small balcony. She waited as Lucas opened the leather case and began taking out file folders, some thick and filled with paper-clipped pages, one thin with the corner of a black-and-white photograph hanging over the edge. A man's hand, the cuff of his shirt torn and frayed where a cuff link had been ripped from its buttonhole. The murderer had taken Alan's diamond cuff links and his watch and pen, too.

The realization hit her hard. That was Alan's hand she was looking at. *His dead hand.* Mattie shuddered. "Are those pictures of the murder scene…of Alan's body?"

"Yes," Lucas said, watching her closely. "You don't have to look at them if you don't want to."

"I…I don't think I can," she whispered. Alan, good-natured, his voice sometimes overloud if he'd forgotten to put in his hearing aids. He'd lost his hearing after years of working around engines without ear protection but his handicap never slowed him down.

Lucas picked up the folder and put it back in the case. "He died almost instantly, Mattie," he said quietly. "The knife blade severed an artery. He probably never even had a chance to call for help."

"He shouldn't have had to call for help at all," Mattie said fiercely. "He should have been perfectly safe in that hallway. I hope Nathan sues the hotel for every penny he can get."

"I don't know what he intends to do," he said carefully. "Do you?"

"I haven't spoken to Nathan for several weeks. You don't have any reason to question him again, do you?" Lucas had cast a wide net in the first weeks after Alan's murder. Alan's son, Nathan, had briefly fallen under suspicion as had a number of others.

"His alibi's airtight."

"I knew it would be." She relaxed slightly. "Alan and Nathan had their differences like many fathers and sons, but deep down they loved each other very much."

He tapped the thick folder with the tip of his finger. "Here are copies of all the interviews I've had with NASCAR people. I've sorted out the hotel staff. They've all checked out. Some of them might have problems with Immigration but they're not suspects."

"But someone connected with NASCAR is?"

"It's the most logical path to follow. The kitchen staff was employed by the hotel, that's their policy. But Grace Winters was on the books as the official caterer. She only brought two or three of her staff to New York in an advisory capacity."

"That was probably her brother-in-law, Tony Winters," Mattie said, making a face. She'd run into the man once or twice and didn't like him much. "They're supposed to be partners in her business, but from what I've heard he's not much of an asset."

"Yeah," Lucas said. "He hasn't got a criminal record, at least not one that's surfaced, but his credit's shaky. He seems to have a habit of living beyond his means. Don't know why she keeps him around."

"For her family's sake, I suppose," Mattie said, leafing through the typed pages. Each of them contained a photo of the subject and a page of vital statistics. She was probably going to be up half the night reading them. "Grace's father and brother are well thought of in the racing business. I never met her late husband but I never heard a bad word spoken of him. Tony benefits from their goodwill, I suppose you'd call it."

"I've included my own notes," Lucas said. "Go ahead and add anything you might think of. I'd appreciate a fresh perspective."

Mattie wrinkled her nose. "Am I going to find lots of embarrassing details about my friends' lives in there?"

He shrugged. "You might." His gaze was challenging. "You must come across sensitive subjects when you're digging for information for your investigations. How do you handle it?"

"If it's pertinent, I include it. If it isn't, I don't," she said, giving him back look for look.

"Same here, I suspect."

It wasn't the same. The people she investigated for her stories were strangers. This file contained information on her friends…and family. Lucas had interviewed her father that night, just like all the others.

"You aren't going to lose your nerve on me, are you?"

"No."

"Good." He reached into the briefcase one more time and pulled out a small leather-bound book with the initials *A.C.* stamped on the front in gold lettering.

Mattie reached out and smoothed the tip of her finger over the monogram. "This is Alan's day planner. He was never without it. He always said he couldn't remember something five minutes after it happened so he wrote down everything here." Mattie felt her throat close and tears filled her eyes. She blinked them away.

"May I?" she asked, unsure of the protocol for handling evidence in a murder case.

Lucas picked it up and handed it to her. "It's been gone over with a fine-tooth comb."

She thumbed through the pages, the hairs on the back of her neck rising as she tried not to feel as if she was invading her old friend's privacy. Alan had been dead for almost eight months. This might be their last chance to find his killer and bring him to justice. It was no time to be squeamish or sentimental. She sniffed back the tears and concentrated on the letters and numbers on the pages.

Alan used the little book as both a day planner and a journal. Alongside appointments with his doctor, accountant and investment broker were little jottings on the weather, or a particularly interesting article he'd read in the newspaper and wanted to pass along to friends, reminders of his great-nieces' and nephews' birthdays, bits and pieces of his life that stopped abruptly with a cryptic notation: "ask D about G."

"Ask D about G?" she murmured aloud.

"Nathan Cargill figured it meant ask Dean Grosso about Granola-Plus. They'd discussed a possible sponsorship earlier on the day of the banquet. Dean Grosso also remembers seeing Alan make a notation in his journal while they were all seated at the table after the banquet."

"Granola-Plus? That's one of those health bars isn't it? Supposed to be good for you but still loaded with calories."

"Yep, that's it.

"Rumor had it they were interested in an associate sponsorship for Dean's car this season but the deal fell through when they found out he was retiring. I didn't hear if they made a play to get Kent to switch sponsors after he left FastMax for Cargill-Grosso Racing."

Lucas shrugged broad shoulders. "Don't ask me about the ins and outs of NASCAR sponsorship. What I overheard between your father and stepmother and that Tieri guy last weekend is the extent of my insider knowledge." His mouth quirked up at the corner a fraction of an inch and she found herself smiling in return.

"Then again maybe 'ask D about G' doesn't have

anything to do with Granola-Plus. Maybe Alan wanted to ask Dean Grosso about something else." A skitter of nervous excitement danced across her skin. "Maybe it means ask Dean about Gina. Is it possible Alan learned something about Gina Grosso's kidnapping and he wanted to talk to Dean about it?"

"Hard to know," he said, not joining in her excitement. "There's no other notation but that one. Grosso said their conversation that evening didn't include anything memorable or out of the ordinary."

"Still, it could be about Gina."

"Like I just said, Dean Grosso was adamant he didn't discuss the kidnapping with Alan at all that night. Sorry."

The little spurt of excitement faded away, leaving her feeling tired and drained. She was jet-lagged and suddenly overwhelmed by the amount of information Lucas had thrown at her. She felt like crying all over again, almost did when she flipped back a page or two in Alan's journal and saw a note he'd written reminding himself to give her a call to make a date for lunch.

"He was going to invite me to lunch," she said. "He never had a chance to make the call. I never got to say goodbye." Horrified, she watched a tear fall onto the page, blotting her name. She blinked hard but the tears wouldn't go away.

She looked up. Lucas's face swam out of focus. She didn't care anymore if he saw her cry. "I am going to stick with this until we find who killed him," she said. "Who do you want to talk to first?"

CHAPTER SEVEN

"THIS ISN'T WHAT I HAD in mind when you asked me who I wanted to talk to first," Lucas said, eyeing the racing helmet Mattie held out to him with suspicion.

"You wanted to see NASCAR people in their natural surroundings, didn't you? Wanted them to be open and relaxed, right?"

"That was the plan."

"You made a good start last weekend at the race. They aren't as wary as they used to be, but now it's time to take the next step. Bonding, if you want to call it that."

He took the helmet, turning it over in his hands. It was black and shiny and looked as though it would be a tight fit. A couple of substantial scuffs on the temples showed it had gotten some use in its lifetime. "What do I need this for?"

"Might as well start with the people who were closest to Alan—my godparents, Patsy and Dean. We're going to the Farm," Mattie told him, reaching into her closet to bring out a similar blue helmet for herself. "We're going to do some karting and then we're having dinner with the Grossos. All of them."

"What's the Farm?"

"Juliana and Milo's home. Dean and Patsy live there,

too. It's a beautiful old place about half an hour from here, outside Concord. Kent and Justin built a kart track there to race on their off days."

"They race go-karts on their days off? Isn't being strapped into a race car every week enough for these guys?"

"It's a great way to let off steam and competitive as hell. Just what the doctor ordered, and since the race is here in Charlotte this week everyone's got a little more downtime to fill. You'll like it."

"I've never been in a go-kart."

"Don't try and snow me, Haines," she said saucily. "I looked you up on the Internet. You were with the MPs in Iraq and Afghanistan. I bet you did some off-road driving overseas."

"More than I wanted to," he said grimly. Chasing down joyriding Marines in an armored jeep was one thing, sitting four inches off the ground, going forty miles an hour on a dirt course was something else. He hadn't figured she'd turn the tables on him so quickly. He'd spent most of the day reading her articles, researching her background, surfing the NASCAR blogs for mentions of her and her famous father. Of Steve Clayton he found plenty but his daughter kept a much-lower profile.

They took her car, a hybrid SUV, and for the most part drove in silence, except when Mattie pointed out something of interest she wanted him to note. He didn't mind letting her drive. He'd told her that before. He enjoyed seeing the countryside, still green and summer-like even though they were halfway through October.

Mattie reminded him a little of the car they were driving. She was something of a hybrid. A woman who had been raised in an eclectic atmosphere. Upper West Side penthouses and summers in the Hamptons when she was with her upwardly mobile mother, and the more casual world of NASCAR when she was with her race car driver father. In Mattie's teen years, her mother had married an Italian count of dubious lineage, and her father had left racing to try his hand at wine making and Mattie had continued to bounce back and forth between the two of them, one semester in an exclusive finishing school in Connecticut, the next in a Mooresville high school.

By the time she was twenty-one, Mattie was out on her own, on her way to becoming a well-respected investigative reporter. He had thought she chose the subject of professional and college sports because of her father's athletic background, but seeing the gleam in her eye as she contemplated an afternoon of kart racing made him reassess his conclusion.

He watched her drive from the corner of his eye as they sped along the rolling low country back roads. She drove fast, but not recklessly, slowing a little when they passed another car or pickup truck, lifting her fingers off the steering wheel in a friendly little wave that was always returned, if not already initiated by the other driver.

"Folks are friendly out here," he commented, having had enough of the silence, wanting to hear the faint Southern drawl underlying her every word.

"They are that," she said. "I imagine you're more accustomed to a one-finger salute from drivers in the city." She turned her head and grinned at him. "Am I right?"

"Driving in Manhattan does tend to bring out the worst in people," he agreed.

"It doesn't bother you to let a woman drive?" she asked, turning her attention back to the road.

"Not if they drive as well as you do."

She smiled more broadly. "I had a good teacher."

"Your dad?"

The smile disappeared. "No, my godfather. My dad was too busy getting the vineyard up and running to teach me to drive."

"Okay," he said. "Sore spot there."

"Want me to ask you a question about your mom?"

"Point taken." He crossed his hands behind his head and leaned back against the seat.

"Sorry," she said. "I try not to let it show but you're right. It's still a sore spot. I hope my dad doesn't make the same mistakes with the new baby when it gets here."

"Do you know if it's a girl or a boy?"

"No," she said, after a moment, adding a little sheepishly, "I haven't asked."

"Maybe you should." He had to remember she was thin-skinned about her relationship with her famous father. Hell, he shouldn't be giving her advice on how to handle the new baby's arrival. His own family had been dysfunctional with a capital *D*.

She chose not to respond. "Here we are," she said as they turned into a tree-lined lane between stone pillars whose wrought iron gate was already open. Horses grazed behind white fences on one side of the driveway, a slow-moving creek followed beside them on the other.

"Milo raises quarter horses," she explained as they pulled into a space in front of a ten-bay garage with what appeared to be living quarters tucked under its high, steep roof. Half a dozen trucks and SUVs were arrayed along the garage's length, all high-end, all

American made. Most NASCAR drivers portrayed themselves as down-home, guy-next-door types, but Lucas wasn't fooled. A lot of them were that, but they were also millionaire businessmen and competitive athletes in a sport where even one moment with a lack of focus could result in disaster. But could one of them be a cold-blooded murderer, as well?

"Milo also collects antique cars. He's got some beauties in here." Mattie kept talking, oblivious to his momentary lack of concentration. "I'm sure he'll show them to you if you ask."

"Milo is Dean Grosso's grandfather, correct?"

"Yes. He's ninety-three and as sharp as a tack, so don't make the mistake of talking down to him."

"I wouldn't dream of it," he said, reaching into the backseat of the SUV for the duffel bag holding the helmets.

"He's one of the last of the founding generation of NASCAR still living. He was there at the beginning, when they used to race on the sand at Daytona Beach and figuring in the tide was part of your racing strategy. Before that, he was an FBI agent. He actually met J. Edgar Hoover. I was always jealous of Sophia for that. My dad's grandfathers both worked in a cotton mill and one of my mother's was a butcher in Kansas City, although she'd die of embarrassment if any of her friends knew that."

"My mother's grandfathers were immigrant German farmers who barely spoke English. We found out one of my dad's ancestors was a horse thief who left Ireland just ahead of the law. My mom was so embarrassed she tried to get Dad to cross the guy's name off the family tree." She laughed as he'd intended her to. "I'm looking forward to seeing Milo again."

"You interviewed him this summer?"

"Yes. He and Kent left the banquet early by the service elevator and avoided the bottleneck outside the ballroom caused by the out-of-order elevator. There was no need to bother Mr. Grosso with any questions on the night of the murder."

"He and Alan were friends for many years," she said, inclining her head in the direction of a small rise behind the house. "That's where we're headed." They started walking. "Milo knew Alan as well as anyone alive, and his wife, Juliana, knows everyone in NASCAR."

"I'd like to speak to her."

"Don't worry. You'll be kneeling at her feet like the rest of us when you taste her lasagna."

"That experience I'm definitely looking forward to."

Six or eight people could be seen standing at the top of the rise as they approached. The figures, mostly male, although he recognized Sophia Murphy and her mother among them, were silhouetted against the blue October sky. The noise of small gasoline engines revving proclaimed the kart track to be on the other side of the hill, still out of sight.

"Like I just said, Milo was there at the beginning of NASCAR. He can tell you anything you might want to know about the old days." Her expressive eyes darkened for a moment. "Maybe the killer is someone from Alan's past, someone who held a grudge all these years and picked the banquet to settle the score."

"It's possible," he said. "Anything's possible."

Her chin came up. "You're making fun of me."

"I'm not," he assured her grimly. "If the motive for Alan's murder wasn't simple robbery then it has to be something else. Bad feelings from the past are as good a reason as any to kill a man."

LUCAS WAS BEING A GOOD SPORT about the ribbing he was taking for running his kart off the track and halfway under the fence, Mattie decided. He'd startled Milo's prize mare into a headlong gallop across her pasture and brought a rain of hoots and catcalls down on his head from the spectator's gallery. He'd levered himself out of the small, ground-hugging vehicle, waved his hand in acknowledgment of the good-natured insults, dusted the dirt and grass off his jeans and, once the kart was jockeyed back on the track, he'd gunned the small motor to life and finished the course.

Dean and Patsy had watched with Mattie as the incident unfolded. Her godfather, his arms crossed on his chest, his eyes narrowed against the setting sun, was silent, showing neither approval nor disapproval of Lucas's behavior. Patsy, always more demonstrative, clapped encouragement as Lucas rolled back onto the course. Sophia reached over and gave Mattie a hug.

"He's got grit," she said, laughing. "Most men would give up and go sulking off to the showers if they got run off the course by a woman."

It had been Sophia's aunt Crystal, her uncle Larry's new wife, who had forced Lucas off the track on the hairpin turn that followed the angle of the pasture fence. Larry, a professor of mathematics, had taken over the job of score keeping from Patsy when he was eliminated in the second heat. Sophia's cousin Steve, Kent's spotter, was standing with his father. His girlfriend was a veterinarian and an emergency surgery had kept her from joining the family outing.

"Someone should tell Lucas that Crystal's been driving go-karts since she was a kid." Patsy laughed. "He didn't have a chance against her."

"He'll get over it. We'll make your city-slicker boyfriend a part of NASCAR nation before you know it," Sophia teased.

Mattie ignored the now-familiar stab of guilty conscience she felt whenever her pseudo romance was mentioned. Somehow it didn't sound quite as ridiculous as it should have to hear Sophia talk as if Mattie and Lucas had a long and happy future in front of them. She had better watch herself. She had a tendency to talk herself into falling in love with unsuitable men, and Lucas Haines was one of the most unsuitable of all.

"Let's hitch a ride back to the house with Granddad. I want to wash this engine stink off before we eat dinner." Sophia and Mattie had held their own in the short sprints that began the afternoon's racing, finishing second and third behind Kent, a former NASCAR Sprint Cup Series champion, but had wrecked each other in the first round of full-course racing.

Lucas, a steady, competent driver, had made it to the semifinal round before being eliminated. After his wipeout, Justin and Crystal had gone on to battle their way to a tie for an old short-track trophy of Milo's that had somehow morphed into the Holy Grail of kart racing in the Grosso family.

Milo had joined them for the last fifteen minutes or so of competition, driving out from the house in his golf cart, watching from the comfort of its driver's seat. "Tell them boys to wind it down," he yelled at Dean and Patsy. "Juliana's beginning to fuss that dinner will be spoiled."

"We're coming, Granddad." Sophia jogged over to

the old man's side and leaned under the golf cart's canopy, planting a kiss on the top of his bald head. Everyone called Juliana Nana, but only Sophia referred to the Grosso family patriarch as Granddad. To everyone else he was Milo.

"Mattie, why don't you and I ride with Milo," Patsy suggested, coming up to link arms with the younger woman. "We haven't had a chance for any girl talk for weeks and weeks. I want to hear all about what's going on in your life." She gave a quick glance over her shoulder toward the group of men gathered around the low-slung go-karts. "Everything."

Mattie's heart sank. She was going to have to lie to her godmother, or at least dance around the truth, to keep this evening from turning into a disaster. She plastered a smile on her face. "Great, I'd love to." Sophia had already slid onto the seat beside her great-grandfather. Thankfully Sophia kept up a lively chatter during the short ride to the house, saving Mattie from being asked questions she'd rather not answer.

They entered the century-old farmhouse through the back door, the entrance the family used. It opened onto an enclosed porch that spanned most of the width of the house. Part laundry room, part entryway, it in turn led to the heart of the home, Juliana's kitchen. Mattie couldn't remember a time she'd visited that this big, high-ceilinged room wasn't filled with the smell of good food and happy voices.

Mattie knew those memories weren't entirely accurate. The Grossos had had more than their share of tragedy and difficult times over the years, but the underlying love and warmth the family shared always seemed to be what lingered in her memory and in her heart.

"Nana," she said, moving forward to be enveloped in a hug by Sophia's great-grandmother. Juliana was in her midseventies but she seemed younger to Mattie. She was always busy, always talking, always the center of whatever was going on. She had met Milo while she was singing in a bar in Nashville. He was a widower, older than her, but like Sophia, once Juliana had decided Milo was the man for her, there was no turning back. Mattie would like to find that kind of all-or-nothing love. She didn't hold out much hope of it ever happening to her, though, especially not as long as she was embroiled in a make-believe romance with a totally not-her-type New York cop.

"Mattie. Welcome, welcome," Juliana sang out, a myriad of gold and silver bracelets jingling on her wrists. "It's been too long. What have you been doing with yourself?"

"I'm so glad to be here, Nana," Mattie said, returning the hug with genuine affection. "Thank you for inviting us."

"Us," Juliana repeated, eyebrows raised as she looked past Mattie's shoulder. "Where is this young man you've brought with you? I want to meet him."

"He'll be along, Nana," Sophia chimed in, hovering over a huge tray of antipasti sitting on the black granite island in the middle of the kitchen.

"A police detective, from New York, Patsy tells me. Not your usual type," Juliana said archly. She slapped Sophia's fingers playfully. "Wait for the others."

"Nana, I'm starved. Beating the pants off the guys out there worked up an appetite." She held up her hand for a high-five from Mattie. "We smoked them, Nana."

"Shame on you two. You know you've been driving

those karts since you were twelve. You shouldn't show off so."

"We weren't showing off," Sophia said with a wicked, saucy grin. "We are just better drivers than they are, but don't you dare tell Justin I said that. Besides we took ourselves out of the running for the trophy on the first heat just to even things up."

Juliana laughed, and Mattie found herself laughing, too. "I wouldn't dream of it. Now shoo! Mattie, you and I will catch up after dinner. Go, talk to Milo for a little while. He loves to flirt with pretty girls."

"Yes, Nana," Mattie said, conscience pricking once more. Then she told herself to stop being so squeamish—the ends justified the means in this case. The people in this room wanted to see Alan's murderer brought to justice as much as she did.

She crossed the room to the seating area that was Milo's private fiefdom. The furniture was old, well-worn leather, the stone fireplace darkened from years of winter fires, the big windows that flanked it looking out over the pasture where Milo's prized quarter horses grazed in the lingering fall twilight.

Milo was sitting in his favorite recliner, scrolling through the channels on a big-screen TV. She came up behind him, rested her hands on his stooped shoulders and dropped a kiss on the top of his head just as Sophia had done. He lifted a bony hand and covered her left hand with his. "Mattie girl, come sit with me." He muted the TV and patted the arm of the recliner next to his.

She perched on the edge of the seat. "How are you, Milo?"

"Upright and taking nourishment," he shot back. "At my age that is quite an accomplishment."

"It sounds to me as if you could use a glass of wine," she said, knowing how the old man enjoyed a glass before dinner. "I brought a bottle of dad's Cabernet. I think you'll like it."

"Of course I'll like it. Your dad's turned into a first-rate winemaker. Don't just sit there, Mattie. Open it. Let it breathe." He leaned back in his recliner, a smile stretching his lips. "A glass of good wine is one of the few pleasures I have left."

"I heard that," Juliana called from her island command post.

"And the love of my life by my side," Milo added with a wink to Mattie.

"That's better," his soul mate said with a laugh from the kitchen.

Another pang arrowed through Mattie. She would give all she had on earth to find a love like Milo and Juliana had shared for almost fifty years. But such a love was rare, and so far she had been an abysmal failure at her search.

It seemed to Mattie that everyone in the world she knew was pairing up these days, foremost of all, her never-get-serious-about-a-woman father. She felt lonely and left out, but then the back door opened and the Grosso family poured into the room. Mattie found she was holding her breath, waiting, watching, not for her godfather or Kent or Larry, but for the other male in the group.

Lucas, dark hair tousled and still damp from washing up in the laundry room, leather jacket slung over his shoulder by one finger, blue eyes sharp and observant, at odds with his relaxed stance and easy self-assurance as he accepted a cold bottle of beer from Kent, kicked her heart rate into overdrive.

It was just a natural reaction she told herself. She was a healthy female with a healthy libido. Lucas was the kind of man that turned women's heads, the kind of man that could turn Mattie's head if she wasn't careful. He looked over at her, studied her face for a moment, smiled at her, then lifted his bottle in a silent salute.

And damn it, she smiled back. Grinned like a fool, was more like it. She jerked her eyes away, concentrated on picking up Milo's glass and taking it to him, but not before she saw Juliana and Sophia exchange a quick glance and a knowing smile. Mattie felt her fingers and toes go icy cold as the significance of the exchange hit her like a blow. It was the kind of smile women exchanged who knew another of their kind was falling in love.

CHAPTER EIGHT

"I TOLD MILO FOR THE HUNDREDTH time yesterday that he has to do something about those cars of his. Half a dozen of them. None of them worth anything." Juliana rolled her eyes as she spoke. "I mean, they're not high-end luxury cars or anything like that. Why, he still has the '60 Chevy he owned when we first met. Imagine."

"I intend to keep that car until I have no earthly use for it," Milo grumbled from the other end of the table. "That car's special to me. We had our first date in that car."

"Stubborn old man." Juliana waved her fingers in feigned protest, but she looked pleased despite their bickering. In Lucas's family a difference of opinion like that would have escalated into an argument or at best a cold, strained silence. Here, in this large gregarious family, it caused only a momentary stir and was quickly forgotten as conversation resumed.

Mattie leaned both elbows on the table, her hands cupped around a glass of wine, a smile curving her mouth as she stared down into its ruby depths. If Lucas wasn't coming to know her moods and personality quirks so well, he would think she was merely enjoying the conviviality of an evening among old friends. But damn it, he *was* beginning to know how her mind worked and she wasn't content and happy. She was nervous and on edge and he was the reason why.

The Grossos were good people. Mattie's father and her new stepmother, too, as far as that went. He was being an ass forcing her to lie to them about their relationship, even if it was mostly by omission. But he still didn't see any other way to have worked himself into the center of their circle—sitting across the table from NASCAR Sprint Cup Series champion Dean Grosso, on the right hand of his formidable grandmother—in less than a week's time after being stonewalled by their clannishness for the past six months.

"Another slice of tiramisu, Lucas?" the grand dame of NASCAR asked with what he already recognized as deceptive mildness.

"I think I could find a spot for a small one," he said, taking his cue. The smile she'd bestowed on him with studied politeness turned genuine, lighting her brown eyes, giving him a glimpse of the stunner she must have been in her prime.

"I like a man with a healthy appetite."

"Keeping up with the Grossos tends to give a city boy like me an appetite," he responded, nodding his thanks as she slid a very large piece of the mouthwatering, espresso-laced dessert onto his plate.

"You weren't bad out there for your first time behind the wheel of a go-kart," Dean admitted, waving off his second piece of dessert with an apologetic smile for his grandmother. No, technically she was his stepgrandmother. Juliana was Milo's second wife.

"I enjoyed myself," he said, lifting a bite of cake to his mouth. "I kept thinking it was just like driving in Manhattan in miniature."

Dean grinned and Juliana laughed aloud, patting his arm. "Good answer," she said approvingly.

On the surface the Grossos might look as though they were living the American dream, but this family had also suffered the heartache of early deaths and a lost baby. Milo's thoughts must have been following the same track, because he suddenly demanded, from the head of the table.

"What are you doing about finding the bastard that killed my friend?"

Lucas turned and faced the old man's scowl. "Everything I can, sir."

"It's been almost a year since Alan died. I'm ninety-three years old. I want to see whoever did it behind bars before my Maker calls me home."

Mattie, who was seated on the old man's right, put her hand over his bony fist. "Lucas is following up on every clue he can find," she said soothingly.

Milo snorted. "Girlie, that line is as old as police work. Even back in my day that meant we had no idea in hell who did it." He gave Lucas a hard stare. "I was an FBI agent in my time. Anyone tell you that?"

"Yes, sir," Lucas said. "I know that very well."

"Then come clean," the old man said, leaning back in his chair. "Bring us up to date."

Everyone else had stopped eating and was watching him. Mattie was watching him, too.

"It is true most of my leads have dried up," he admitted. "But that's good news, too. Some of the earliest possible suspects were people you know, Nathan Cargill for example."

"It was ridiculous to even suspect Nathan for a moment," Patsy said in the absent man's behalf. "We couldn't have completed the sale of Cargill Motorsports if it hadn't been for him."

"Close family members are always suspect, not to mention that he's the one who found the body. Nathan and Alan were known to have butted heads in the past."

"But they'd put all that behind them. They were very close the last few months of Alan's life. Nathan says that was a great comfort to him."

"He had an airtight alibi," Dean said, picking up his spoon to stir his coffee.

"An alibi he was unable to substantiate for some time after his father's death," Lucas corrected.

Milo narrowed his eyes and hunched his shoulders, giving his bald head something of the look of a turtle pulling back into his shell. "Who else was on your list?" he demanded.

Lucas decided to lay his cards on the table. It was what he'd promised Mattie the other night on the plane. "Brent Sanford, a former NASCAR driver who left the sport under a cloud."

"Brent wasn't the one who messed with Kent's car," Larry said in a quiet voice that no less demanded attention. "It was a fired crew member who was the culprit. Alan admitted he was wrong that night. He intended to apologize to Brent. He told my brother so before… before he died."

"Brent wasn't in the hotel at the time," Dean pointed out.

"To anyone's knowledge," Lucas corrected the older man. "You and your wife, however, were ideally situated to commit the crime."

Juliana gasped and opened her mouth to say something. Mattie, too, looked as if she intended to give him a piece of her mind, but Kent Grosso, first off the mark, beat them to it. "What the hell," he said, leaning forward from across the table. "Are you saying my parents were at one time considered suspects?"

"Business associates score a close second to family members when we're looking at possible suspects," Lucas said, returning the former NASCAR champion's challenging gaze. "But your parents never left the ballroom. They were still there when the body was discovered."

"Good Lord, next you'll be saying Milo was on the list because he was one of Alan's oldest friends."

Lucas lifted his hand from the tablecloth, acknowledging the accuracy of the statement. "You and your great-grandfather left the ballroom fifteen minutes ahead of the time Alan Cargill excused himself from the table where all of you, plus several others—Grace Winters, who was catering the banquet, and Adam Sanford, of Sanford Racing, to name two—were seated. You did, however, leave the room through the same doorway Alan used, the one opening into the service hallway, enough right there to warrant putting your alibi under extra scrutiny."

"We told you we took the service elevator because one of the others wasn't working and there was a long wait. Granddad was tired," Kent explained, his jaw set stubbornly.

"The hotel's beverage manager remembers escorting you to the service elevator and descending with you to the hotel basement where he then led you to a secondary elevator that returned you to your suite, on the seventeenth floor if I am remembering correctly. I don't have my notes with me."

Mattie was watching him with narrowed eyes. Everyone else was, too. Kent held the challenging eye contact for a half minute longer then relaxed, rested his elbows on the table and steepled his fingers. "Okay. You got me there. Who else of our friends did you think you could pin it on?"

Lucas didn't take offense at the confrontational tone. He'd react the same way if their situations were reversed. "Grace Winters, as I said, was overseeing the food service from the kitchen that accessed the hallway."

"But she was there with us at the table when the murder occurred," Patsy reminded him, looking pleased that she'd tripped him up.

"Yes," he said. "You all share the same alibi. But there were several other members of her staff who came with her from Charlotte to oversee the banquet. Not all of them have stellar reputations."

"Tony Winters," Sophia said immediately. "That guy gives me the creeps."

"He's something of a loose screw if you ask me." Kent glanced at his sister, then gave a short nod. "All kinds of rumors floating around the circuit where that guy's concerned."

Lucas felt the short hairs at the nape of his neck begin to stir. He didn't dare look at Mattie but kept his attention focused on the man across the table. This is what he'd been waiting for. This was the kind of small talk and casual reminiscences that might lead him to a new line of questioning, a new detail, a new opening in the dead end Alan's murder investigation had become.

"When Justin and I were planning our wedding reception with Grace, Tony gave me the willies every time he showed up."

"What do you mean?" Mattie asked. Lucas saw her fingers tighten slightly on the stem of her wineglass.

Sophia wrinkled her nose. "He's just too full of himself. Too loud, too enthusiastic... You know, like one of those late-night TV pitchmen trying to get you to believe you can't live without whatever it is they're selling."

"And there have been rumors about his lifestyle." Juliana added a detail of her own. "It was about the time Grace's husband passed, remember? Talk of drugs and gambling and such. Never came to anything that I know of, but you hear these things."

"He doesn't have any criminal record," Lucas said carefully. That didn't mean the guy wasn't dirty. It just meant that he was good at not getting caught.

"Like I said, it was just gossip," Juliana said, picking up her coffee cup, the gold and silver of her bracelets chiming with each movement of her hand. "Everyone was talking about the Winters family at the time. Grace being left with three babies and all. Todd Winters was very well liked. His dying so young and so suddenly was a terrible thing. His mother, Susan, was devastated. But Tony just kept going off and leaving Grace and his mother. Trips to the Indian casinos and Biloxi and Atlantic City. And not winning, either, if my sources are right, and they usually are." She raised her coffee cup to her lips. "Shameful behavior, if you ask me, especially for an accountant. There's no way on earth Milo or I would trust him with any of our business." She set the coffee cup down with an indignant thump.

Justin added, "Tony's a strange one, all right. Talked Grace into taking him into her business and then never showed up most times when we did meet with her, just like Sophia said. He works for Matheson Racing, too.

Claimed to be putting in a lot of overtime or something. I don't remember."

"I don't think he's working for Matheson anymore. I can't recall who told me that," Larry interjected. "I'll see if I can scrape up any more details."

"Thanks," Lucas said.

"The jerk crapped out on Grace the day of our wedding, too. Left her to do all the work herself," Justin said with an edge to his voice.

"The reception went off without a hitch," Sophia said loyally. "Grace is an absolute genius at what she does. That's why NASCAR insisted she be allowed to oversee the banquet in New York, even though it was against hotel policy. What about the hotel employees? Couldn't it be one of them? After all, Alan was robbed of all his things. Isn't that why you decided it was just a crime…of…what do you call it?" She glanced around the table, her blue eyes settling on Mattie's face as she lifted her hands in a helpless gesture.

"A crime of opportunity," Mattie supplied. "As I understand it that was the only conclusion the police could draw when all of the hotel employees and all the guests' alibis checked out."

"She's right," Lucas said, wishing he could have kept them going in the direction of Tony Winters, but Sophia had changed the dynamics of the conversation and he didn't want to give any of them the idea he'd moved Grace Winters's brother-in-law a long way up his list. "There had been a couple of random muggings in the hotel in the weeks before Alan's murder. In the absence of any substantial evidence, it was logical to assume he was another victim of the mugger."

"You guys never even found the murder weapon,"

Dean Grosso said. "Or anything with Alan's blood on it."

"It isn't as easy as it looks on TV. If the murderer had access to the kitchen, the murder weapon could have gone directly into the dishwasher, which would eliminate any physical evidence."

"Was it ever determined if the weapon was a kitchen knife?" Patsy wanted to know.

Lucas shook his head. "No. The weapon could have been a kitchen knife, a long slender one, like a fillet knife. Or it could have been a switchblade, easily concealed."

"Alan bled to death," Dean said, giving his grandmother an apologetic look. "Wouldn't the murderer have had blood on his clothes?"

"Not necessarily. Due to the position of the body in the stairwell the bleeding was mostly internal. Any stained clothing could have been pushed into a cart and trundled off to the hotel laundry before the police arrived."

"My money's still on someone from the kitchen," Kent said, as stubborn and opinionated as the rest of the family.

"As I said, the hotel's staff checks out. A few of them may have trouble with immigration issues but as far as NYPD is concerned they are all in the clear. As is the street thief, Armando Mueller, who was caught fencing Alan's fountain pen. We're keeping our eye on him in case he leads us to someone higher up the food chain, but he's no longer a suspect."

The same could no longer be said of Tony Winters. Lucas hadn't made contact with the Charlotte police for a couple of weeks. Until now he'd taken them at their word that no one on his NASCAR list had a criminal record, but maybe it was time he asked for a little more detailed background information on the celebrity chef's brother-in-law.

"Enough of this kind of talk," Juliana said, taking control of the table. She raised her glass for a toast. "To Alan," she said as the others followed suit. "May he rest in peace."

After they drank the toast, silence descended on the room. Lucas found himself staring into Mattie's troubled brown eyes. For a moment their gazes caught and held. He had gone as far as he could go that evening. If he pressed harder, he risked the progress he had made gaining the confidence of the close-knit Grosso clan. If there was any more information to be gained, it would have to come from Mattie's efforts.

"Nana," she said as though reading his mind. "There's one more thing I would like to ask all of you about Alan before we leave this room." There was a slight catch in her voice and Lucas knew she was close to tears.

"What, Mattie?" Juliana asked as Milo leaned closer so that he could hear what she had to say.

"Yes, what is it, Mattie girl?"

"Lucas showed me Alan's journal," she said, fixing her gaze on the old man's time-worn face. "You remember his journal. He was never without it. He had it with him the night he died. One of the last things he wrote concerned this family," she said. Patsy stretched out her hand. Mattie linked fingers with her godmother across the width of the table.

"Mattie, don't bring this up, please," Patsy begged.

"I have to, Aunt Patsy," she said, begging in return.

"We have no idea what that entry in Alan's journal meant," Dean said, his voice low and whiskey-rough around the edges.

Mattie nodded, turning to face Dean, one hand still entwined with Patsy's, the other clasped in Sophia's. "Yes, I know. Lucas told me you had discussed it. But are you sure it meant, ask Dean about Granola-Plus, not…ask Dean about Gina?"

He sighed, looking grim and sad but completely convinced of what he said next. "Yes, I am. Alan would never have needed a reminder to talk to us about Gina. He was there with me when I got the news from the hospital that she had been taken. He was always there for us. Mattie, think about it. Use that first-class brain of yours, not your heart." The smile he gave Mattie was bittersweet. Lucas saw Patsy Grosso's fingers tighten convulsively in Mattie's.

"He wouldn't have waited a moment to tell us if he had learned something about our baby's kidnapping, Mattie, dear. Dean and I have discussed this before…many times. Whatever that cryptic phrase meant to Alan it had nothing to do with her, with the rumors or the mysterious person writing that blog that insists she's alive and somehow connected with NASCAR, nothing at all."

"You're sure?" Mattie's eyes swam with tears that she seemed determined to hold at bay. "You're really sure?"

Patsy and Dean exchanged glances. "Yes, Mattie, God help us, we're sure."

CHAPTER NINE

"I BLEW IT, DIDN'T I?" Mattie asked, clenching her hands tightly on the steering wheel, her expression troubled in the glow of the dash lights.

"I wouldn't say you blew it," Lucas replied carefully. The gathering hadn't broken up immediately after Mattie's insertion of Gina's kidnapping into the conversational mix; the Grossos were far too well mannered for that. But within half an hour they were on their way back to the city, early-morning appointments and media interviews for Dean and Kent being the excuse for ending the evening.

"You don't have to be diplomatic about it. I ruined your chance at getting any more details out of any of them."

They were riding with the windows down. He could smell leaves burning and see the pinprick glow of a bonfire off in the distance. "I was done asking questions," he said. "The more emotional people get about a subject the less objective they become about their memories."

"Thanks for trying to give me an excuse. I apologize. It was a rookie mistake."

"Quit beating yourself up. You've surely done interviews with skittish subjects before? You're the one who keeps telling me police work and investigative reporting are a lot alike. Sometimes you get what you want. Sometimes you don't."

"Was any of what they told you helpful?" she asked. She wouldn't have liked it if she'd known he could hear the faint note of pleading in her voice.

"Not a lot," he said, careful to be as truthful as possible. They were coming into the outskirts of Charlotte. Traffic was picking up and streetlights replaced the moon-glow outside the car window. He was sorry for that. He liked to see the silvery light reflected in Mattie's hair and the star-shine sparkling in her brown eyes.

"I was afraid of that." A rueful smile lurked at the edges of her mouth. "I've watched so many crime scene investigation shows on TV. I figured you guys would be able to find trace evidence—" she lifted her right hand from the steering wheel "—I don't know, just drifting around in thin air, I guess. Especially after Alan's cuff links were found at Patsy's party."

"No prints. No DNA," he said shortly. "Clean as a whistle."

He braced one knee on the dash and leaned back against the seat, striving to keep his mind on the subject at hand and not on how kissable her mouth was. It was getting harder and harder to keep his mind on his job around Mattie. Damned hard. "Those guys on TV make it look easy. They get all the breaks. Never make a mistake. Never overlook a piece of evidence or not figure out a witness is lying through his teeth. It's always case solved and scenes from next week's episode all neat and tidy in sixty minutes flat."

"With time out for commercials."

That surprised a laugh out of him. "Yeah. Superheroes. All of them." He hesitated, and then went with his gut. "There was one thing."

"Yes?" They were stopped for a red light. She turned to face him.

"Justin Murphy mentioned there were rumors of gambling and drug problems connected with Tony Winters. Dealing or using?"

"I haven't a clue," she admitted.

"What do you know about this guy?"

"Not a lot more than you heard tonight. He's older than I am. Midthirties or so. His brother, Grace's husband, was the oldest in the family. Great guy. Everyone liked Todd. Tony hangs around on the edges of NASCAR. Works part-time for Matheson Racing—in their offices, not at the track."

"From what they said tonight he doesn't even have that connection to racing anymore."

"Guess that's right, too. I've met him once or twice." She wrinkled her nose. "Like Sophia said, he's just too friendly. Talks too loud, laughs too hard. Always in your space, if not in your face. You know the type."

They had turned onto her street and into the alley that led to the small parking area behind her apartment. "He's caught your interest, hasn't he? I know my antennae came out during that dinner conversation. It happens anytime I hear the words *drugs* and *gambling* in the same sentence. What makes you think it might be him after all these months?"

"Pretty much the same as you, drugs and gambling." Lucas shrugged as he unsnapped his seat belt and got out of the car.

Mattie looked at him over the hood of her SUV. "Alan's cuff links turning up at Patsy Grosso's birthday party last month turned conventional wisdom upside down, right?"

"Right. No New York street thief or hotel mugger was on the guest list. It was strictly A-list."

"And Tony Winters was there because of Grace."

"According to the Grossos, Winters has more bad habits than I was initially led to believe. Gambling and drug dealing usually means money's involved. Guys who owe money to those kinds of people get desperate pretty quick when they need to pay what they owe. That gives him an extra star on my list."

"Tony was there the night of the murder. He had access to the kitchen and the knives," Mattie said, excitement tingeing her words. "But he must have had a good alibi or you wouldn't have let him go that night."

"Grace Winters was his alibi, but it sounds as if she's used to taking up the slack where's he's concerned."

"Grace would never cover up a crime," Mattie said earnestly. "I mean, I don't know her all that well, either, but I've never heard a bad word spoken about her."

"I'm not saying she's done anything wrong. I'm just saying it was a very busy, very stressful night. Time tends to get away from you in those circumstances, gets out of sync. She could have lost track of her brother-in-law for ten or fifteen minutes and never even realized it. Winters could have confronted Alan in the stairwell, stabbed him, washed his hands, disposed of the knife and returned to the party in that amount of time."

"I suppose." Mattie moved around the car as they talked. Now she stood toe to toe with him, her head tilted slightly so she could look him straight in the eye. She smelled good and the warmth of her skin eddied between them, making him itch to reach out and take her in his arms. "Tell me the truth, do you believe Tony Winters killed Alan?"

"Slow down," he said, giving in to temptation and taking her by the shoulders. "I didn't say any such thing."

"But you're suspicious of him, aren't you?"

"I think it's worth giving him a second look," he agreed cautiously. He would make a courtesy call to his contact in the Charlotte police department first thing in the morning. It was true Tony Winters had no formal arrest record but maybe, just maybe, the cop could substantiate a few of the details Lucas had learned about the Winters family's black sheep this evening.

"You think more than that," she said, putting both hands on his chest, giving him back look for look. "I've been around you long enough now that my X-ray vision can penetrate that thick shell of macho-cop armor you wear. C'mon. We're partners, remember? Tell me what you're thinking." She raised her face to his, her eyes shining, her expression intense, committed, alluring as hell.

"I'm thinking of kissing you," he said, and did.

MATTIE OPENED HER MOUTH to protest, but that was obviously what he was waiting for. His tongue swooped inside, probed and cajoled, demanded she kiss him back. And she did. Her arms slid up his hard, muscled chest, wrapped around his neck. She let her fingers play through the soft hair at his nape, something she'd been aching to do for almost as long as she'd known him.

She let him pull her closer, mold their bodies together. His arms were hard, his chest was hard. He was hard all over and she gloried in the contrast against her own soft curves. She felt as if she'd been made for just this purpose, to be held and kissed almost senseless. She giggled at the fanciful, politically incorrect notion. Women didn't admit to wanting to be kissed senseless these days, but she couldn't help herself. Lucas raised his mouth a fraction of an inch. His hair was like silk beneath her fingers. His breath was warm against her lips. He smelled of some kind of spicy aftershave and leather. He tasted of espresso and fine red wine. She wanted to cuddle even closer. "What's so funny," he said.

"Nothing," she whispered. "Just a silly thought that flashed through my head."

"What's flashing through my head is that I want you very much," he said, and kissed her again.

This time Mattie had herself under control, well, almost under control. She didn't feel like swooning, but she did feel like doing a great many other things with Lucas. Dangerous, irresponsible things that would lead to heartache and rejection, just as her other love affairs in the past had ended. She didn't feel sexy and romantic anymore. She felt scared.

When the kiss ended she unwound her arms from around his neck and took a step back, putting a little distance between them, welcoming the swirl of fresh night air that cooled her blood and helped clear her thoughts. "My neighbors might be watching," she said, holding him off.

"I can fix that." He pulled her into the shadow of the tall, narrow building.

"Nothing's broken," she said, her hand on his chest keeping him from taking her in his arms again. The narrowness of her escape left her more breathless than the kiss. She had come close to losing all restraint with this man. She hadn't allowed that to happen for a long, long time. "But there might be if we don't slow down." Her heart would be what broke. It was full of little cracks already, like an old piece of china. She didn't think it could take another blow like the ones she'd suffered in the past. "I think we should call it a night."

"What's wrong?" he asked. "Are you sorry you let me kiss you?"

"I didn't let you kiss me. We kissed each other," she shot back. "No, I'm not sorry. I just don't think it's wise to take it any further."

"Do you want to take it further?"

"No," she said but her heart and her body said yes. She ignored both entities. "Remember this dating thing is just a front for your investigation. It's not supposed to get any more serious than being seen in public together."

"Sophia and Juliana don't seem to share that sentiment. They're matchmakers, both of them. I could spot them a mile away."

"Of course they are. Sophia's been studying at her great-grandmother's knee since we were both in grade school. Juliana is as good a matchmaker as she is a cook."

He took a step backward. "Then I'll be on my guard," he said. She couldn't read his expression but she could hear a sudden wariness in his voice, as if he, too, were having second thoughts about that mind-blowing kiss.

The second one they'd shared, she remembered suddenly. The first that night at her father's house, had been more of a challenge, a dare. This one? This one had been in another league entirely.

"What are you going to do to follow up your hunch on Tony Winters?" she asked as he walked her to the door. They didn't touch this time. He was careful to keep distance between them, too, she noticed.

"I'm going to touch base with my contact in the Charlotte P.D.," he said as she fished for her keys in her shoulder bag. She'd left the duffel with the racing helmets in the trunk of her car. She'd deal with it in the morning.

"You'll let me know what you find out."

"Don't get your hopes up, Mattie. So far Tony Winters is just a name that came up in conversation tonight. That's all."

"I'm going to go over the transcripts of those interview tapes you gave me. Maybe a fresh eye is what they need."

"It can't hurt."

"And the Gina Grosso blogs. I'm going back through them, too."

"Why?" he asked, leaning against the pillar of her tiny back porch.

She lifted her shoulders in a shrug. "I don't know," she said. "I'm almost certain Alan was referring to baby Gina in that last message in his journal. Maybe he heard something, or saw something that related to the kidnapping. Something that occurred during the banquet. He had to have made that notation just before he died."

"No one recalls seeing him writing in his journal."

"He was always doing it. No one remembers because it was such a familiar sight. A habit. Don't ask me how I know it was what he meant. I just do."

"This isn't some kind of 'woo-woo' psychic feeling, is it?" he asked, just a hint of a smile curving his mouth.

"No," she said, lifting her chin. "No 'woo-woo' psychic stuff. I'll admit it's a hunch, a good old-fashioned gut feeling."

"Feminine intuition, maybe?"

She canted her head a little to one side. "Why not? It's a time-honored tradition. Or used to be."

He traced the curve of her jaw with the tip of his finger. It took all Mattie's willpower to keep from shivering at his touch. "Okay. I can go along with that. I act on my gut feelings once in a while, myself. In fact, I did a while ago. I'd like to do it again."

"But you're not going to," she said, turning the key in the lock and stepping inside her apartment. "Because we both know it's better if we don't. Good night, Lucas."

"Good night, Mattie," he said, walking away, his shoulders broad against the darkness.

She touched her finger to her lips very lightly. She had told him it was better if they didn't kiss again. Her logical brain had spoken those words, but her traitorous heart felt differently. It told her the kiss had been very, very right.

CHAPTER TEN

"MATTIE, IT'S ME, SARAH. Am I interrupting you?"

"No, of course not. What can I do for you?" Mattie tucked her phone against her cheek and poured a cup of coffee. It was midmorning, the day after the dinner at the Grosso farm. Mattie was still in her pajamas but already on her second pot of coffee and her second stack of interview folders.

"I…" Her new stepmother hesitated as if choosing her words with care. "I'm going to be in your neighborhood this afternoon doing some shopping. I hoped you might be able to join me. My friends are giving me a baby shower and—" Again the slight hesitation in the other woman's voice.

"I know. I've been invited," Mattie interjected as she gazed out her window at the dreary October morning. She hoped the rainy weather didn't last much longer. Qualifying for Sunday's race began that afternoon.

"You have? Why how nice. I hope you plan to attend." Sarah sounded genuinely pleased that Mattie had been included. Mattie's conscience pricked her for her attempts to think up an excuse to back out of the party.

"I wouldn't miss it," she heard herself say so she couldn't weasel out later.

"I'm going to register at the layette shop on your

street this afternoon. Everyone says they have very nice things there."

"They do," Mattie said. "I pass by it all the time. I'm free today. I'd like to join you." She said it very quickly so she couldn't weasel out on that, either. She hadn't heard from Lucas yet today. She wondered if he was already meeting with his contact in the Charlotte police department. She wished she had more to tell him from her own research, but she hadn't come across anything that jumped out at her and screamed *You missed it. It was right here all along. Tony Winters killed Alan Cargill.*

"Excellent." Sarah sounded relieved. "I have a faculty meeting at noon but I could be there by two o'clock. Will that work with your schedule?"

"It will work fine." They said their goodbyes and hung up.

Mattie had several more hours for her continuing Internet searches, and she intended to use every minute of them to good purpose because the night before she'd accomplished nothing—zilch, zero, nada—despite her telling Lucas she intended to work long into the small hours of the morning. She'd spent the entire remainder of the evening berating herself for having given in to her attraction—fast turning into all-out infatuation—for the New York detective.

Her dreams, when she did manage to fall asleep long after midnight, had been even more troubling, explicitly sensual, erotic even. She was getting in way over her head. But how could she step back from him now, at least in their unholy alliance to find Alan's killer? That bond she couldn't break, but she certainly intended to conduct herself more circumspectly in the future.

She was still brooding over what had transpired when

she met Sarah outside the baby boutique. Her stepmother was carrying a utilitarian black umbrella unfurled to protect her from the misting rain that had persisted into the afternoon. Mattie was in jeans and a cotton sweater in shades of gold and copper, her favorite colors. Sarah was wearing a light fall jacket and tailored slacks over a tunic-style shirt, not exactly maternity wear but coming close. She was barely showing, a small baby bump you could hardly notice, but what wasn't hard to notice was the way Sarah carried herself. The "pride of pregnancy" she thought Shakespeare had called it.

"Hi, Mattie. Have you been waiting long? I should have told you we'd meet at the wine shop across the street. You'll be bored silly looking at baby things," Sarah apologized before Mattie could deny she'd been waiting longer than a minute or two.

"I like looking at baby things," Mattie said, smiling to put Sarah at ease. "I check out the window displays all the time."

"You do?" Sarah looked relieved and shyly pleased. "I…I haven't had much time for that yet. I have a lot going on at the university, and there's been so much traveling back and forth since your father and I were married." She wasn't looking directly at Mattie as she spoke, but at the tiny pastel garments in the shop window. Sarah's reflection revealed a soft, wistful smile. Mattie shifted her gaze before Sarah could catch her looking. Her stepmother was usually so confident and self-contained it would probably discomfit her to appear so vulnerable.

Mattie took a closer look at the older woman. She hadn't been imagining the fatigue in Sarah's voice. Her stepmother looked pale and tired, almost her true age. "Let's go inside," Mattie said. "I'm sure they have an electronic gift registry. All the stores do along here. You use a scanner like in the supermarket and swipe it over the things you want on your wish list."

"Really? It's that easy?" Sarah asked, her professorial persona back in place as she neatly furled her umbrella and stepped into the boutique with its pale yellow walls and Beatrix Potter murals and polished antique armoires displaying the tiny clothes.

"If it isn't, I'll act as secretary and take notes, and you can just 'ooh' and 'ahh' over all the cute little outfits and rattles, and silver cups and spoons, and whatever else takes your fancy." Sarah was neat as a pin and not a drop of rain marred her hair or her clothes. Mattie, on the other hand, hadn't remembered her umbrella until she was half a block down the street and hadn't gone back for it. Now she could feel the dampness already starting to curl her hair. She groaned. It would be out of control for the rest of the day.

"Baby monitors are a must. I want one for every room in my apartment and then there's the house in Pebble Valley, too. I'll need two or three of everything if Steve and I continue this bicoastal pattern we've developed." She stopped talking and reached out to touch the lacy edge of an elaborately detailed christening gown, the same one Mattie remembered admiring in the window just a week ago—the day Lucas had walked boldly into her life with his audacious suggestion they fabricate a romance for the sake of finding Alan's killer.

"How lovely." She sighed. "So tiny and so beautifully made."

"It is lovely, isn't it?" the salesclerk said, coming up

to greet them. "Mrs. Clayton?" It surprised Mattie a little that Sarah was using her father's name. She had assumed she would remain Professor Stanton. Jumping to conclusions was becoming something of a habit for Mattie these days, and she didn't consider it an attractive trait.

"Yes, I'm Sarah Clayton and this is...Mattie."

The middle-aged, matronly woman nodded. "If you'd like to have a seat I'll show you how our electronic gift registry operates and then the two of you may take all the time you want looking around."

"Excellent," Sarah said briskly, as the clerk turned to lead them toward the back of the store. The smile she gave Mattie was slightly apologetic. "I thought you might appreciate me not introducing you as my stepdaughter. I didn't want to embarrass you." She swept her hand toward her abdomen.

Mattie felt slightly ashamed of herself. She had been standoffish since Sarah married her father. It was time she stopped acting like a spoiled brat. She liked Sarah, what she knew of her. She wanted them to be friends. "Don't be silly," Mattie said, giving Sarah's arm a squeeze. "I wouldn't be embarrassed at all. I'm looking forward to being a big sister again. I'm pretty good at it, actually. Even with the twins, and that's saying something. Are you ready to shop?"

"Yes," Sarah replied. "Let's shop."

Sarah made her choices with her usual efficiency, most of them practical and gender-neutral and a few more whimsical. She'd chosen a unicorn and fairy mobile with dangling prisms that sent rainbows dancing in all directions as it revolved and a cuddly, stuffed panda that Mattie suspected was more for Sarah than the baby.

Sarah looked just a little sheepish as she spun the mobile with the tip of her finger. "Steve and I agreed that we wouldn't find out the baby's sex, but that doesn't mean I'm not hoping for a little girl."

"I suppose Dad wants a boy," Mattie said, surprised how hard it was to keep the statement casual and off-hand as she ran the scanner over a bath set.

"Quite the opposite, he wants another daughter." Sarah gave Mattie another wistful smile. "'A beautiful baby girl, just like my Mattie' is what he said."

"He was probably joking. I was a terrible child," Mattie said to cover her confusion. It was odd to think of her dashing father as a man looking forward to having an infant in his life again. She looked down quickly, careful not to let her emotion show.

"No. He wasn't joking, not at all," Sarah assured her.

Mattie made a decision she hoped wouldn't come back to sear her heart when the overture was rejected. "You've made him very happy. I think he will make a wonderful father this time around. I'm very happy for both of you. I meant it when I said I'm looking forward to being part of a family again."

"I wish you'd tell your father that," Sarah said softly.

"I will," Mattie promised herself as much as Sarah. "Honestly, I will."

"Thank you," Sarah whispered, "for all our sakes."

Mattie nodded. "Oh, look at this cute little outfit," she said when she could trust her voice again.

"Absolutely adorable." Sarah took the cue and didn't pursue the topic of Mattie and Steve's relationship further.

Forty-five minutes later, they walked out of the store with the gifts Sarah had chosen duly noted into the registry. When Sarah had gone to the restroom, Mattie erased the christening gown and the unicorn mobile from the scanner's memory and made arrangements with the saleslady to have them put aside as her personal gifts to the new parents.

It was raining harder and there was a cool autumn feel to the air as they stood on the sidewalk, undecided about what to do next. Sarah opened her umbrella and held it so that Mattie could shelter beneath it, as well. "Let's have a glass of wine before you leave the neighborhood," Mattie invited. "My treat."

Sarah touched her stomach almost shyly. "No wine for me, thanks, but I'd love a glass of iced tea."

"I should have thought of that," Mattie apologized. "No alcohol, right."

"Not exactly. My doctor said I could have a small glass of wine now and then, but all I've been able to eat today were soda crackers and weak tea. I don't think I should drink any wine on an empty stomach. The results could be uncomfortable and embarrassing for both of us."

"I've got an idea. Let's go to the ice-cream parlor instead. They have a great Belgium waffle sundae and my sweet tooth has been nagging me to have one for the last week or so." Mattie hoped the shop's delicious homemade ice cream would tempt Sarah's appetite.

"I'm not sure I can handle all that sugar," Sarah said candidly, paling a little, as if the thought of so much sweetness turned her stomach.

Mattie hesitated. "If you'd rather not—"

"Don't be silly." Sarah gave her an impish grin. "I'm becoming an expert at watching other people eat. I live vicariously through them. And honestly, a little morning sickness will be more than worth it to have a baby of my own."

Just as before, when she'd stood on this very spot gazing at the baby clothes in the window, Mattie's inner voice chimed in. *Me, too,* it said. *Me, too.* She shook off the sudden longing impatiently. Sarah had a husband, a good man to father her baby. Mattie had no one in her life. Well, that wasn't precisely true. She had the suspicion that Lucas would be a good candidate for the job. However, becoming a single mother wasn't on Mattie's life list. She didn't want to raise a child the way she'd been raised, bouncing from house to house, parent to parent, never really feeling grounded in any one place for more than a few months or weeks at a time.

She wanted the whole white-picket-fence-dog-and-kids-in-the-yard kind of family. She wanted to fall in love and stay in love for the rest of her life.

So far that hadn't happened, or more truthfully she hadn't let it happen. She was just too afraid of failing and ending up with a broken heart. She hadn't been attracted to any man enough to take the risk of falling head over heels in love.

Until last week when Lucas Haines had barged into her life.

Deep down inside she was terrified that he just might be the one.

LUCAS HAD OPTED OUT OF parking behind Mattie's apartment building as he had the night before. Instead he fed the meter in the public lot at the end of the street. He needed to walk, to stretch his legs, even if it was still raining. Misting was a more apt term but it was still enough to get you wet if you stood in one spot too long.

He quickened his step as he came in sight of Mattie's building. Her little second-story balcony, barely wide enough for two plastic chairs and a bottle-cap-size table was conspicuously bare of the flower boxes and stoneware containers of plants that decorated the other three balconies in the four-unit building. A testament to her gypsy lifestyle or just a lack of gardening skills? He suspected the former. His own apartment's small terrace was equally barren.

He wondered if she ever wanted to settle down, raise a family, stay in one spot long enough to plant flowers and watch them grow and bloom? He had been thinking more and more along those lines himself since Mattie had become so much a part of his life.

He didn't like the turn his thoughts were taking. He'd promised himself a long time ago that he wasn't going to get married, get tangled up with one woman and then find himself in the cold, adversarial tug-of-war his parents' marriage had been.

Nope. No way. No how.

He was a loner, had been since he was a kid and he intended to keep it that way no matter how deeply Mattie Clayton got under his skin.

A discreet tapping sound caught his attention. He turned his head. Two women were sitting in the window of the old-fashioned-looking ice-cream shop next door to the wine shop where he and Mattie had had their first meeting of the minds.

One of them was dressed in copper and gold, her dark hair a wild halo of curls around her face, the other was also dark haired but more conservatively dressed. It was hard to see any more details through the rain-streaked glass. Nevertheless, he'd know that saucy profile anywhere. Mattie? He looked a little closer. It was Mattie and her stepmother. It was the older woman who had caught his attention by tapping on the glass with the handle of an umbrella. She motioned him inside.

"Lucas, how nice to see you again." Sarah Clayton beamed as he walked up to their table. It was the tail end of a rainy October afternoon. The shop was empty except for one obviously bored college kid behind the counter. He was wearing a white coat and pants and one of those white paper hats that you saw in all the old black-and-white photos of soda jerks from back in the day. The whole shop was done up that way: wrought iron tables and chairs, revolving fans on the ceiling, black-and-white tile on the floors. Behind the counter there were big glass jars of candy and the cloying scent of chocolate fudge hung heavy in the damp air.

"Mattie's treating me to a waffle sundae. I haven't enjoyed anything so much in weeks and weeks."

Lucas glanced down at her dish. The ice cream was melting over the waffle and the hot fudge had congealed around the edges. It looked as if it had barely been touched, but both women seemed pleased with themselves so he had to assume it had been even larger when it came to the table.

He couldn't deduce that by looking at Mattie's portion. Her fluted dish had been licked clean. *She liked hot fudge sundaes as much as she liked Mikey's banana pudding.* He automatically added that detail to his mental catalog of her personality traits.

"Yes, I ate it all, every bite. And if you hadn't ambled by I'd probably be spooning away at Sarah's by now," she said as though she'd somehow gained the ability to read his mind.

"You're welcome to it. I feel fine, but I'm not going to press my luck." Sarah pushed the glass dish toward Mattie.

"I think I will," Mattie said defiantly. She reached out and pulled Sarah's abandoned sundae closer and took a small bite.

"Join us, won't you," Sarah invited after waiting a moment for Mattie to offer the invitation.

"Thanks." He snagged the back of a spindly looking chair and lowered himself gingerly onto the seat. "I bet I'll gain a couple pounds just sitting this close to that sundae," he said with a conspiratorial grin for Sarah. She giggled, flushing a little when Mattie glared at him. He ignored her. "What brings you to Mattie's neighborhood?"

"Shopping," she said, avoiding looking at her stepdaughter, but her eyes sparkled with a teasing glint. She was a very attractive woman when she shed her professorial persona. "My friends at the university are giving me a baby shower. Mattie helped me register at the boutique across the street. They have some lovely things."

"Sounds like an enjoyable way to spend a rainy afternoon," Lucas said, dropping his teasing tone.

"It was very enjoyable for me. I just hope Mattie wasn't too bored."

"I had a ball," Mattie returned with a smile for Sarah. "What did you do with yourself this morning, Lucas?" she asked, a sly gleam in her eye. She knew very well he had planned on touching base with his contact in the Charlotte P.D. She was baiting him. He didn't mind. He knew beneath her veneer of casual interest she was on fire to know the outcome of his visit.

"Catching up on business," he replied, holding her challenging gaze.

"Police business?" Sarah asked, leaning forward in her seat. "Have you learned anything new about Alan's murder?"

Lucas could have kicked himself for even bringing up the subject in front of Sarah. It was unprofessional as hell and another measure of how much having Mattie so close upset his equilibrium and screwed with his mind. "Not much, I'm afraid. I talked to a detective on the department here to see if they'd come up with anything new on the case since Alan's cuff links showed up at Patsy Grosso's birthday party."

Sarah lifted her shoulders as though a little shiver had danced up her spine. "I can't get my mind around the fact that someone related to NASCAR is involved. There's no kidding ourselves any longer that some New York street criminal was responsible, is there?" she asked almost hopefully.

"No," he said, giving her the hard, unvarnished truth. "The killer, or at the least an accomplice to the murder, was at Patsy Grosso's birthday party last month. I intend to use every means at my disposal to find out who that person is."

"And for that you need access to NASCAR," Sarah said, tapping her fingernails on the table. "Mattie's your cover, as you told us that first night at Pebble Valley, but Mattie doesn't have quite the connections I do since I married her father."

"I got Lucas credentialed for the California race. I'm already working on getting him a hard card for Sunday's race, too," Mattie said. He could gain access to the same venues the hard card would get him into through his contact at the Charlotte police department, but he didn't want to go that route.

"Is there anyone in particular you would like to observe?" Sarah held up her hand, palm out. "I don't want to know anything you'd rather keep to yourself, but I would like to help. I never met Alan, but Steve had great respect for the man—" she touched the tips of her fingers to Mattie's "—and I know how special he was to you."

Mattie gave Lucas a quick, questioning look. He nodded slightly, ceding the conversation to her. "There is a suspect. It's no one you know, but we do need tickets to Grace Winters's charity cooking demonstration Friday afternoon. Can you arrange it?" Once more Lucas was surprised by how quickly Mattie had grasped the situation and come up with a plan—what it was he didn't know, but he could almost see the gears whirring inside her very pretty head.

Sarah beamed. "I can. Your father and I bought a table. There are still two seats available."

"Bingo," Mattie said, looking damned pleased with herself as she shot him a grin. "We'll take them."

"Not quite so fast." Lucas switched his attention back to Sarah. She looked slightly apprehensive but determined. "You need to ask your father for the tickets," she asserted. "In person." And then she smiled at Mattie with her heart in her eyes. "Please."

CHAPTER ELEVEN

TWO WEEKS AND A COUPLE OF days ago he'd been sitting in his apartment in an unfashionable section of Manhattan, staring at the window of the apartment across the alley, where every day the old man who lived there lounged in his recliner watching the weather on TV and petting his cat. The cat watched Lucas, too, as it sat on the windowsill and flicked its tail at the brazen pigeons just out of reach beyond the glass. The old man, as far as Lucas knew, never left his apartment for any reason. His own life might come to that. An old age of loneliness and boredom. His family was scattered and not very close. His friends were few outside the department. He was either out chasing bad guys or sitting alone in his apartment. He was coming to realize that wasn't much of a life at all.

Lucas preferred what he was doing now. He grinned, banishing his dark mood. Who wouldn't rather be mingling with the Beautiful People and the NASCAR A-list than watching the weather? Even if he was the only commoner at the table. Mattie was on his left, the daughter of a multimillionaire racing champion and winemaker, an award-winning journalist in her own right. On his other side was the only female driver in this year's NASCAR Sprint Cup Series, Shelly Green.

Beyond her, her billionaire boyfriend, Steve's partner Damon Tieri, the Claytons themselves, and Justin and Sophia Murphy, NASCAR royalty.

He looked up from the square plate of Asian-fusion seared ahi tuna he'd been given by a black-clad waiter and caught Sarah Clayton's eyes on him. Her expression was controlled and benign as always but he saw a flash of kindred feeling in her gaze. "What are we doing here?" she seemed to be asking.

He smiled back. He knew exactly what he was doing here, trying his damnedest to get something tangible on Tony Winters. But it didn't hurt to enjoy his time in the stratosphere while he was waiting for that "something."

They were seated under a tent that had been erected on Victory Lane at the Charlotte race track. At the back, against a backdrop of a giant photograph of the track, a duo of race cars were decked out in the mind-blowing colors of an iconic breakfast cereal and an equally recognizable sports drink, the sponsors of the two drivers involved in the night's festivities. Just in front of the cars, a low stage had been outfitted as a kitchen. Chef Grace Winters, resplendent in her whites and a high, pleated hat, was entertaining the dozen fat-cat donors and their hundred or so guests with a lively stream of chatter and racing anecdotes as she worked her magic with chopping boards and saucepans.

"This is marvelous," Shelly said, smacking her lips as she forked up her last bite of tuna. "Thanks so much for inviting us, Sarah."

"You're welcome, Shelly. It is very good, isn't it?" Lucas had watched as the pregnant woman sampled plate after plate of Chef Winters's creations. A taste of each, that was all, but more food than she had eaten that day at the ice-cream shop.

Everyone at the table spoke quietly so as not to interfere with the show, and for the most part they had limited their communications to lip smacks and eye rolls as sample after sample of time-honored Southern favorites and Grace's own gourmet offerings had appeared in front of them.

The women in attendance were all dressed as though they were dining in the finest of restaurants, the men in suits and ties—not the typical attire for a day at the track. Even the ever-present NASCAR credentials had been tucked away in pockets and tiny, glittery evening purses. Headphones and sturdy shoes and ball caps emblazoned with sponsors' logos, along with the ear-shattering roar of racing V-8s would come later. Now the purpose was to see and be seen and to raise money for a worthy cause. Mattie's dress was black, off the shoulder with a slit in the skirt that left her bare thigh very, very close to his. He shifted uncomfortably and lowered his eyes to his plate. Every time he looked at her he felt his gut tighten with desire.

"I can't eat another bite," she declared, smiling.

"Force yourself," Sophia commanded, eyes fixed on Grace as the chef bantered with the two drivers of the race cars on display, who were acting as her assistants. "She's doing the mimosa sponge cake that's in her cookbook. It is to die for, even Nana says so."

The Grossos, like Steve, were sponsoring a table. Theirs was on the far side of the tent. All the proceeds of the night would go to a charity that coordinated efforts among various law enforcement agencies to help locate missing and exploited children. Lucas had worked with the group once or twice in the past. They did good work, and since the kidnapping of Dean and Patsy's daughter thirty years earlier had become public knowledge, the NASCAR champion and his wife had agreed to lend their support to the cause.

Grace had called attention to Milo Grosso's presence at the event early on in her presentation. The old man had stood slowly and bowed his head graciously to acknowledge the applause. Then Grace had also introduced Juliana, calling on the older woman to come to the island and give the audience a demonstration of how she would deal with the simple pasta dish of heavy cream and freshly grated Parmigiano Reggiano.

Juliana, resplendent in royal blue, her hair in what Lucas was coming to recognize as her trademark French twist, rings and bracelets sparkling in the overhead lights, had proven herself a worthy addition to the evening's entertainment. Standing alongside Grace, dealing with knives and cutting boards with aplomb, instructing the chef to add another clove of garlic, to be generous with the white pepper, promising to send Grace a bottle of her very favorite brand of extra virgin olive oil—which would have made the dish even more delicious, in her opinion—all interspersed with NASCAR anecdotes and little asides on the favorite dishes of half the people sitting in the tables in front of them. The applause when she took her seat had been deafening.

"That's Nana." Sophia grinned. "She steals the show every place she goes."

"Sophia, you mentioned you had a copy of Grace's cookbook a few moments ago. I didn't think it was published yet. How did you obtain it?" Sarah inquired as she spooned a small bite of the lighter-than-air sponge cake into her mouth.

"I have connections."

Sarah lifted her eyebrows. "I'm impressed."

Sophia waved off the praise. "Actually, I went to school with Cassie Connors. She and Ethan Hunt, Grace's brother, are dating." She looked over at Mattie and wrapped her first two fingers around each other. "They keep telling everyone they're just friends but I know better. I predict another NASCAR wedding before the next awards banquet."

"That's the rumor going around the garages," Justin confirmed.

"I'm happy for Ethan. And Cassie is great with his daughter. Sadie's blossomed since Cassie took the job as her nanny."

"Well, I'm blossoming eating this incredible dessert." Sarah laughed and took another bite. Lucas glanced at Steve Clayton. He was watching his wife eat, a pleased and relieved look on his face. Mattie was watching her father and stepmother, too, although trying to appear as if she wasn't. Steve turned his head a fraction of an inch and smiled at his daughter. Mattie smiled back.

Steve leaned toward Mattie. "Sarah hasn't eaten this much in weeks," he said. "She's been feeling better every day since you two went shopping for baby clothes. It seems to have changed her whole attitude."

Mattie reached out and covered his hand with hers. "It's not Sarah who changed her attitude, Dad. It was me."

Steve cut a glance at his wife. She was leaning forward, talking to Shelly Green and Tieri across the table, gesturing with more animation than Lucas had previously seen. "What happened, Mattie?"

"She told me you wanted another little girl," she said simply. "That's all I needed to know."

"I'll be a good father this time, I swear to you. This baby will never get short shrift from me."

"I know she won't."

"I can't change how irresponsibly I behaved when you were a little girl, but can you forgive me for my past sins now that you're grown?"

"I already have."

The diners around them broke into enthusiastic applause and the private moment between Mattie and her father ended. Their table joined in giving Grace a standing ovation as she finished her presentation and came out to walk among the tables and shake hands with the happy and satisfied guests.

When the applause finally died away, they remained standing. "Okay," Mattie said, turning to Lucas once more. Her brown eyes were still shining with the emotion of the shared moment with her father, but she blinked the tears away. She leaned closer, causing him to catch his breath as her light, sexy perfume tickled his nostrils and the low, scooped neckline of her dress gave him a brief glimpse of her softly rounded curves. "Time to go looking for our suspect. He'll be hanging around here somewhere. Excuse us, won't you," she added loudly enough to be heard over the buzz of conversation that had broken out at the other tables. "There are some people I would like Lucas to meet." She gave her father's hand a squeeze. "Thanks for everything, Dad." She smiled at her stepmother. "Sarah. It was great fun, but now it's time for Lucas and I to go to work."

"WHERE ARE YOU TAKING ME?" Lucas asked as they threaded their way between tables. She wished he wasn't quite so close. His aftershave—a natural woodsy scent she couldn't quite place and had no intention of asking him about—was beginning to affect her as though it were some kind of superpotent aphrodisiac. Top that off with a classic black blazer and tie over a midnight-blue shirt that set off his dark hair and eyes and she'd had trouble drawing a full breath when he was sitting so close to her their shoulders almost touched.

"You might as well meet Grace," she said sharply before her imagination could assert itself. She concentrated instead on finding a way to get them inserted into the group around the popular chef. "Tony won't be far away if there's any sign of celebrities or the media. He loves that kind of stuff. I didn't have time to tell you, but I did a slew of Internet searches on the guy over the last couple of days."

A long stretch of time without seeing Lucas, she'd come to realize. They had talked on the phone since he'd left her outside her apartment on that rainy afternoon but they hadn't sat down face-to-face. He had spent most of his time with his contact in the Charlotte P.D., looking through the department's records and compiling a history of Tony Winters over the past ten years. It took time, a lot of time, because a lot of the files weren't computerized yet. She had stayed holed up in her apartment, ordering takeout from the restaurants along her street when she got hungry, her eyes glued to the screen, her fingers flying over the keys as she searched the Web.

Not seeing each other meant there had been no opportunity for him to kiss her again, either, and she was grateful for that. She simply couldn't concentrate when all her senses were focused on the sensual tug-of-war between attraction and wariness that seemed to plague him as much as it did her.

Lucas halted to admire the sleek lines and wildly colorful paint scheme on one of the displayed stock cars. "I'll bet you're trying to figure out how you'd shoehorn yourself into it, aren't you?" she teased.

"Yep," he said laconically. "NASCAR drivers are obviously not prone to claustrophobia."

"If they are, they don't admit it."

"Your stepmother seemed to be feeling better this evening," he said, changing the subject, as several other people arrived to peer inside the race cars, making comments similar to the ones they'd just voiced.

They moved a step or two away as she considered her answer. "I think it's because Dad and I have made an effort to get back on track with each other the past couple of days. I'm ashamed to say I didn't realize how stressful our estrangement was for Sarah. It's been like that between me and my dad for so many years it was just second nature, I guess." She shrugged and ran a pearl-tipped finger along the edge of a sponsor decal. "I can be amazingly selfish when I'm miserable."

"You and your dad talked it out?"

She kept her eyes on the small, colorful and very expensive advertising decal. "We made a start. He was a pretty poor father during the years I was growing up. That's the truth and nothing is going to change it. I was lonely and adrift most of the time." She glanced across the tent to Dean and Patsy's table where Milo and

Juliana were holding court. "NASCAR—these people—were my real family."

"Your dad was a young kid who went from nothing to worldwide fame and tons of money in a couple of years' time."

She liked the way Lucas stood up for her dad. Not because he didn't understand how much Steve had hurt her in the past, but because he was a fair-minded man and understood there were always two sides to every story. "I know that. He was ten years younger than I am now when I was born." She kept her voice pitched low, mindful of the people around them, although for the moment she and Lucas seemed to exist in a small island of privacy beside the stock car. "His second marriage was on the rocks. He had a sullen, lonely preteen dumped on him instead of the sunny little girl who thought spending every weekend camping out at a race track was the perfect lifestyle. It was tough on him. I'm an adult now. I understand why he acted the way he did. But the little girl in me still hurts—" she touched her heart "—right here."

"But not as much as before?"

She looked over at him. He was smiling, but he didn't try and hide the concern in his dark blue eyes. She caught her breath as her heart gave a little jump of longing and desire. She got hold of herself, hoping her emotions were harder to read than his were, and smiled back. "A lot less than it did before."

He reached out and brushed her chin with his knuckles. "Good for you, Mattie." He leaned slightly forward and she wondered if he would kiss her, here, in front of everyone she knew. She didn't care. She wished he would. Not only kiss her but carry her off somewhere quiet and hidden and make love to her. She was tired of playacting. Now, at this moment in time, with the emotions between them so close to the surface, she wanted their relationship to become real. Very, very real.

CHAPTER TWELVE

A DEEP MASCULINE VOICE broke the spell that seemed to have held them separate and alone in the crowded tent of people. “Mattie, it’s good to see you here.”

Ethan Hunt, Trey Sanford’s crew chief and Grace Winters’s adoptive brother came toward them, a petite blond-haired woman at his side. Mattie wondered for a moment what kind of scandal it would bring down on the Hunt and Winters families if Tony was the murderer of Alan Cargill. She hadn’t thought of that before now. She didn’t want to think about it. She couldn’t or she might falter in her quest to bring his murderer to justice.

“Ethan. It’s great to see you, too.” The Sanford Racing crew chief was a reserved man, not given to public displays of affection. Mattie didn’t make the mistake of giving him a hug.

“I don’t think you’ve been introduced to Sadie’s new friend and mine,” Ethan continued, smiling down at the small woman at his side. “Cassie Connors. This is Mattie Clayton. She’s a member of the Fourth Estate but one of the good guys.”

“Nice to meet you.” Cassie held out her hand. “I’ve read some of your articles. Glad to see there’s someone out there holding big college athletics to a higher standard.” Sophia had said the woman was a former United

States Marine. Cassie didn't look big enough to pass the physical, but Mattie didn't underestimate her because of her size. There was more than one kind of strength. From the firmness of her handshake and the straightforward look in her eye Mattie figured Cassie Connors had enough strength of character to make up for any lack in muscle mass.

"Thanks, Cassie," Mattie said, a little uncomfortable as she always was when someone praised her writing. "You've met Lucas Haines before, haven't you, Ethan?"

"Briefly. In New York."

"Good to see you again, Chief Hunt," Lucas said, reserve in his low voice. Mattie noticed Lucas didn't ask Ethan to call him by his first name. It reminded her that he considered himself on the case.

"Detective Haines." Ethan's response was equally formal. It was obvious from the slight, skeptical frown between his dark brows that Trey Sanford's crew chief wasn't going to warm up to an outsider in their midst anytime soon.

"Where's Sadie?" Mattie asked a little too brightly. Ethan's eleven-year-old daughter was a particular favorite around the track. Mattie had always had a soft spot for the motherless little girl. She had been happy to see Ethan bringing Sadie to the races over the last season instead of leaving her with his late wife's parents all year. She suspected Cassie, Sadie's nanny, had a lot to do with it.

"Her grandparents are visiting. Sadie has a new puppy to take care of, so they're spending the evening at our—" she flushed prettily "—at Ethan's house."

"Sounds like Sadie's having fun this evening, too." Mattie caught Cassie's slip but pretended not to. She had always liked Ethan, taciturn and moody as he sometimes was. If Cassie Connors was the woman he'd chosen to spend the rest of his life with, she was happy for him.

The crowd around Grace had thinned a little. The Grossos were still talking with her. Mattie spotted Ethan's father and Grace's adoptive dad, Dan Hunt, standing beside her, his arm around her shoulders. Once more Mattie's conscience pricked her. Dan's wife, Grace's mother, had died suddenly less than a year ago. They were still mourning her loss. Grace would have yet more grief to deal with if Tony truly was Alan's murderer.

Another man—shorter, thinner, with carefully styled brown hair, wearing a dark purple shirt and matching silk tie—more or less elbowed his way into the group around Grace. Tony Winters. Mattie had seen several pictures online, showing him in much the same position, at Grace's side, basking in her limelight.

"C'mon," she whispered to Lucas, her pulse rate speeding up a little. "The game's afoot."

"What?"

"Never mind." She reached out and tugged on Lucas's hand. Her reaction to Tony Winters paled beside her body's reaction to touching Lucas again. For a moment the shock of skin against skin took her breath away, but she swallowed hard and ignored the tingles running up and down her arm. "We'll see y'all later," she managed to croak. "I want to congratulate Grace before she makes her getaway."

"Nice to have met you," Cassie called as Mattie took off with Lucas in tow.

"What's going on?"

"Tony Winters. There he is beside Grace. Let's go. I want to look him straight in the eye and learn what it's like to be face-to-face with a murderer."

"Mattie, don't show our hand," Lucas warned.

"Don't worry. Butter won't melt in my mouth."

"Grace." Mattie sailed into the small group around the chef. She and Grace were the same age. They'd gone to high school together her senior year. Mattie had been a real hardnose in those days. She hadn't made friends easily, but Grace Hunt had always been friendly despite Mattie's rebellious, don't-give-a-damn attitude. She'd always appreciated that, but never felt close enough to the other woman to tell her so. Now she wished she had. "Great show. Great food. Can't wait for the cookbook to come out. If the recipes you served tonight came from it I'll have to buy a copy for everyone I know."

Grace laughed. "Thanks, Mattie. I hope everyone feels the way you do."

"I know I sure do," Dan said heartily, giving Grace a squeeze. "She's dedicating it to all of us who were her guinea pigs."

"Taste subjects, Dad," Grace said, giving him a little punch on the arm.

"Whatever you want to call it, it's the best job I've ever had." Everyone laughed and Dan laughed, too. "Sorry, Grace, honey. I have to run. I'm meeting some of the guys at the Sanford hauler. Might be an opening out there for a broken-down old crew chief next season. You never know."

Grace reached up and gave him a kiss on the cheek. "Good night, Dad. Thanks for coming."

"Wouldn't miss it for the world, honey. Not for the

world." Dan and Grace had a great relationship. Mattie hoped she and her dad could develop one equally as close. They'd made a good start the last couple of weeks. She intended to keep working at it in the future. Something else about Dan and Grace tugged at the back of Mattie's thoughts but she couldn't quite bring it into focus.

The tenuous idea disappeared from her mind altogether as she watched Tony Winters sidle his way closer to the center of the group and take Dan's place at Grace's side. He looked relaxed and mellow and completely guilt free. Maybe they were on the wrong track, she thought with a sharp pang. If she had murdered a man and saw the police detective in charge of the case standing not six feet away, she would have turned tail and run. But then, she wasn't a murderer. Or even an expert on how one behaved. What did she know? She plastered a big smile on her face.

"Grace, you've met Lucas Haines before in his professional capacity, but I'd like to reintroduce him tonight as a friend," she said, hoping her smile didn't appear as forced as the light tone of her voice was.

"Hello, Detective Haines," Grace said, her gray eyes holding the same slight wariness Mattie had noticed in Ethan's.

Lucas held out his hand. "Please, call me Lucas. I'm not Detective Haines tonight, just another of your fans."

Grace continued to study him for a moment or two, the wariness remaining in her expression, before accepting his handshake. "Thank you, Lucas," she said, her smile turning gracious and breathtaking at the same moment. "It's a pleasure to see you again in happier circumstances. And please, call me Grace."

"My pleasure."

A jolt of jealousy slammed through Mattie as she watched Lucas clasp Grace's hand between his own and smile down at her just the way he smiled at Mattie. The emotional blast shook her to the core of her being. She was never jealous. Never. It wasn't her style. Lucas wasn't even really her boyfriend. He kissed like a hero from a romance novel, sure, and she was becoming addicted to those kisses, she'd admit that. But in real life, in her heart, he meant nothing to her.

No. She was too honest to lie to herself that way. Lucas did mean something to her. He meant a lot, and she was afraid she had gone almost too far to turn back where her poor, battered heart was concerned.

While Mattie was recovering from her unpleasant encounter with the green-eyed monster, Sophia and Patsy had made their way to Grace's side. Sophia threw her arms around Grace and hugged her exuberantly. Patsy was more restrained but her face was wreathed in smiles as she congratulated the younger woman on her presentation and her help in raising thousands of dollars for the cause they were sponsoring.

"Pictures," Sophia called out. "Dad? Mattie? Someone have a camera? I want a picture of Mom and me with Grace. Where's Nana? She should be here, too."

"Nana and Milo left to go home. Milo's got a pregnant mare he wants to check on back at the farm," Dean hollered back.

"Mattie?"

"I have my cell phone. Will that do?"

"It will have to." Mattie worked her way closer to the trio of women. She could feel Lucas close behind her, shielding her from the crowd. Sophia and Patsy and

Grace, all three used to posing for fans and media alike, moved close together and wrapped their arms around each other's waists. "How's this?" Sophia warbled.

"Great. Hang on." Mattie clicked off three quick shots, then paused a moment to save them to the phone's memory card, a habit she'd developed after some really great candid shots of one of her subjects had gone missing in cyberspace. "Good. All good."

"Looks like we have three Graces here tonight instead of just one," Tony Winters said, appearing at Mattie's elbow. "I'd like to see those shots, if you don't mind?"

He'd moved from Grace's side to Mattie's so quickly and unobtrusively it gave her a start. "Sure, no problem." Mattie handed over her cell. Her hand was shaking. She couldn't help herself.

The trio of women disbanded. Grace moved on to accept congratulations from other guests. Sophia and her mother joined a group that included Ethan and Cassie and Ethan's boss, Adam Sanford.

"Great shots," Tony said. "Oh, hey. Jeez, I'm sorry. I must have pushed the wrong key. It's gone?"

Mattie all but snatched back her phone. Sure enough the screen where the picture should have been was blank. "What did you do?

"Yeah, Winters, what did you do?" Mattie glanced to her left. Justin Murphy had come alongside Lucas, almost, she thought fancifully, as if he were standing guard over her, too. It was a silly, but comforting thought. Or maybe it wasn't so silly. Maybe the Grossos had put two and two together that night at the Farm and come up with Tony Winters as the prime suspect in Alan's murder, just as she and Lucas had. "I wanted a copy of that picture of my wife," Justin growled.

"It was an accident. Sorry," Tony muttered, although he didn't look a bit sorry to Mattie.

"Don't worry. I took three shots and saved them as soon as I took them. I'll e-mail y'all copies in the morning," Mattie said, not wanting Justin, who wasn't known for his subtlety, to tip their hand to Winters.

Tony's eyes narrowed slightly and Mattie shivered at the cold anger that flashed in his gaze, but he grinned in apparent relief. "Great. I feel better now. I'm a klutz. What else can I say?"

"What's going on?" Grace asked, coming up to the group. Justin put his arm around her and gave her a quick hug.

"Fantastic job tonight, Grace. I know my mom and dad, our whole family, appreciates your making this night such a success."

She reached up on tiptoe and gave him a kiss on the cheek. "I'd do anything for you guys, you know that, especially to help missing kids. My children are the most important thing in the world to me. I don't know what I'd do if something happened to one of them." Her voice thickened with tears and she brushed her fingers across her cheeks. "See. I get all choked up just thinking about it."

"Grace we need to get moving. We were due in the owner's suite ten minutes ago." Tony spoke loudly enough for everyone around him to hear where they were headed as he laid his hand on Grace's arm and began urging her toward the exit.

Grace flushed slightly and nodded apologetically to them all. "There's no rest for the wicked."

Mattie felt her eyes drawn involuntarily toward Grace's brother-in-law. The overhead lights caught the gleam of gold as the cuff of his shirt revealed what looked like a very expensive watch. Rumors on the Internet had hinted that Grace's catering business was having money problems like a lot of others in the economic downturn. If it was, it certainly didn't seem to have affected Tony's lifestyle. Mattie lifted her eyes. He was watching her watch him, a look of purely male satisfaction in his eyes, but beneath that there was something dark and unnerving.

Inside she cringed, but outwardly she stretched her mouth into a smile and pretended not to notice his scrutiny. "I'll e-mail you a copy of the pictures, Grace," she promised, pleased to see Tony's self-satisfied look replaced with a frown. Why didn't he want Grace to have the picture of herself with Sophia and Patsy? A shot like that would be worth a lot if it were hung where prospective customers could see it. He was part owner in Grace's business. Her success was his success, so why try to sabotage it that way?

Mattie filed Tony's strange response away in her memory. She'd think about it later when she had time to mull over the possible reasons for what she now considered a deliberate attempt to erase the pictures from her cell phone. She began to move in the same direction that Tony and Grace were heading, not even looking back, trusting Lucas to be right behind her.

He was. "Where are we going?" he asked, as they exited the tent into the cool, cloudy October evening.

"We'll let him think we're headed to Dad's suite. It's only a few doors down from where Grace and her creep of a brother-in-law are going. I'd like to get a little one-on-one time with him."

"Mattie, you've done great so far this evening but don't spook him."

"Don't worry. I just want to look him straight in the eye and... Never mind."

She lengthened her stride. The race track was relatively quiet, the infield camping area only beginning to fill with motor homes. The work day at the track was nearly over. NASCAR mandated the garages and haulers be locked down after a specified time each evening. They were coming close to that curfew. The clatter of wrenches and hammers being placed in toolboxes, and the sounds of men's voices calling out to each other followed them past the brightly lit, spotlessly clean bays. Off in the distance Mattie could hear more male voices coming from the backs of the mammoth haulers where most of the teams were gathered for their evening meals. The smell of charcoal smoke and grilling meat perfumed the air. Her stomach rumbled despite all she'd eaten such a short time ago. She was a real Low Country girl when it came to appreciating barbecue.

"Grace, Tony, wait up a moment," she called as their quarry halted at a Club Car they evidently intended to use to take them to the tower above the grandstand that housed the VIP suites. "Can Lucas and I hitch a ride? I want to show him the view of the track from Dad's suite."

"We're in a bit of a hurry," Tony said shortly. "Grace has an interview—"

"Don't be silly, Tony," Grace interrupted with an apologetic look. "There's plenty of room. Hop in, you two."

Tony drove as quickly as the small vehicle would travel, causing the electric engine to whine in protest and making conversation difficult. Mattie sat beside

Lucas in the rear seat and fumed. She was so impatient to question Tony Winters that she could almost ignore the heat of Lucas's hard thigh against her own. Almost.

They crossed under the track through the pedestrian tunnel and emerged near the main building where the VIP suites and Speedway Club were located on the upper levels. They all entered the elevator together, but Tony looked as if he wished he could close the door on Mattie and Lucas.

"Are you going to be here for the race Saturday night?" Mattie asked, masking her probe for information as small talk, as she watched the numbers on the digital display inside the elevator climb toward their destination.

"Yes," Grace said, sighing a little. "But I'm not looking forward to it."

"We're doing some publicity stills for the cookbook Saturday," Tony said importantly, emphasizing the *we*.

Grace made a little face. "My least favorite part of the business. Especially when it takes time away from my kids. Don't get me wrong. I loved what we did tonight. It's so much fun to interact with my audience. And Nana was fantastic. I wonder if she'd agree to come on my show?"

Mattie smiled at the thought of the flamboyant Juliana on a nationally syndicated TV cooking show. "She'd be sensational and probably end up with a TV show of her own."

"Grace, we're keeping everyone waiting," Tony interjected as if he didn't want to hear any more speculation on how successful Juliana Grosso might be competing against Grace.

"All right," Grace said without much enthusiasm.

"I imagine you have a tight deadline with the book coming out next year."

"Yes, and Tony's going on vacation soon, too, so we need to get this done."

Mattie swiveled her head to look over her shoulder. She channeled her mother in her überhostess persona and smiled up into eyes that did not smile back. "Where are you off to, Tony?" she asked, considering the effect of batting her eyelashes at him before deciding against it. He was already suspicious of her attaching herself to him and Grace this way. No need to make him more so by overdoing the friendliness.

"Costa Rica," he said.

"How lovely." Mattie's insides tightened. Did Costa Rica have an extradition treaty with the U.S.? Even if it did, it would be easy enough to disappear in a place like that. Go native, they used to call it and never be heard from again. "Is it an ecotour? Are you into bird-watching? Are you going deep-sea fishing? Or volcano watching?" She heard herself start to babble and closed her mouth so quickly her teeth snapped together.

"No," he said, giving Mattie a long, hard stare as the elevator doors opened onto a sweeping view of the race track and the fading sunset beyond the grandstands. "I don't really have an itinerary planned out. I'm just going to kick back on a deserted beach somewhere and live the good life."

"How long will you be gone?" she asked as they prepared to go their separate ways.

"I don't know," he said, his smile never reaching his eyes. "I might like it so well I never come back."

CHAPTER THIRTEEN

"DID YOU HEAR HIM?" Mattie asked. "He says he might never come back. Do we have an extradition treaty with Costa Rica?"

"Yes," Lucas replied grimly. For what it was worth. If the Costa Rican authorities weren't in the mood to cooperate with the U.S. it could take years to get a prisoner back to the States. If, and it was a big *if,* the fugitive was ever caught in the first place.

"We've got to stop him. We've got to do something." He and Mattie had parted from Grace and Tony Winters at the elevator. She had taken Lucas to her father's VIP suite and they had dutifully stared out at the darkened track for all of thirty seconds before leaving the building. They were standing in the shadows of the big race complex, arguing about what to do next. She was tense and wired by their encounter with Tony. He could feel her vibrating with eagerness and anxiety. "Can't you put a tail on him? Take him in for questioning? Arrest him for jaywalking or littering or something?"

"Mattie. Stop. Take a deep breath. Settle down." The darkness and her nearness made him reckless. He reached out and took her by the shoulders and gave her a little shake. "I thought you told me you didn't get overly emotional about your subjects," he said, trying not to let himself think about his dad and the gung-ho reporter that cost him his job and ultimately his life. "You're always objective, always a step removed, remember?"

She stiffened beneath his hands, then sucked in her breath and let it out in a whoosh. "I am. I'm all those things. I told you the truth. Investigative reporting is my job, not my calling. But this—this is different. Alan wasn't some spoiled, pot-smoking college quarterback, or greedy coach turning a blind eye when fat-cat alumni passed out freebies. He was special. He was my friend." Her voice broke a little, and he felt like a cad for letting his own bitterness get the best of him, even for a moment. "We can't let him get away with it." A tear slipped down her cheek.

He felt as if he'd been stabbed in the gut. Mattie didn't cry. He felt helpless and clumsy, unable to comfort her. "Get in the car," he said gruffly to hide his own emotions. "And don't cry."

"I'm not crying. I'm angry," she said, but did as he told her. He pulled out of the speedway grounds and into traffic, heavier than he was used to at this time of day, as motor homes and campers began arriving at the campgrounds surrounding the race complex in anticipation of the weekend's competition.

"Where are we going?" Mattie asked.

"To my hotel," he said. "I need to make some calls if we're going to have any chance of taking Winters into custody before he leaves the country."

"How are you planning to do that?"

"I wish I knew." She lapsed into silence again, but he could see by the way she clenched her hands on her purse that she was still keyed up. "Look, the important thing is to act as natural as possible. Don't make him suspicious."

"And you probably don't really trail all that many suspects, right?"

"I've been known to keep one or two under surveillance in my time," he said. "But I'm out of my territory here."

"They haven't seemed all that interested in him so far is what you're saying."

"That about sums up the situation."

"We're on our own."

"More or less."

She nodded as they pulled into the hotel's parking lot and headed for the side entrance he'd been using all week. He swiped his room card and held the heavy glass door for her to pass through. "You aren't even going to buy me a drink at the bar before you take me up to your room?" she asked, slicing him a glance from the corner of her eye.

He was relieved to see her sass was back. He didn't like to admit how it churned his gut to see her unhappy or upset. "I thought you might not want to be seen going up to my room with me. This is your stomping ground. There might be someone in the lobby who knows you, or who recognizes you as Steve Clayton's daughter. Besides, there's a minibar in my room."

"Thanks," she said, looking pleased that he'd thought of her reputation. That surprised him a little. He figured she would go the gung-ho feminist route and declare it was no one's damned business but her own whether she visited a man's hotel room or not. Just another difference between North Carolina and New York. Southern manners won out over political correctness every time. He kind of liked that.

"I could use a glass of something," she admitted with a little sigh.

"There's beer in there. And a couple of little bottles of wine. None of your dad's, though, I'm afraid." He wasn't much of a drinker, maybe because he had seen what misery alcohol abuse had caused in the lives of too many of his fellow cops.

"I was thinking more along the lines of bottled water."

"That I can handle. The French stuff, even."

"I'm impressed," she said, sailing into the elevator ahead of him, giving him a view of her rounded backside and the curve of her bare thigh as the skirt of her slinky black dress swirled around her. He dragged his eyes away from the low neckline as she bent forward, her finger poised on the keypad. It struck him that the reason he should be worried about her reputation was that he didn't want her to be seen *leaving* his room in the small hours of the morning in that dress. "What floor are you on?"

"Four," he said, telling himself to take a breath before he passed out on the floor.

"Going up," she said, giving him a dazzling smile. It wasn't only the elevator that was rising, Lucas thought. So was his desire to take her in his arms and make love to her.

The room he was calling home these days was big, with plenty of space to move around. There was a couch and a comfortable chair, a flat-screen TV, a table big enough to allow him to spread out his case notes and files alongside his laptop. Mattie crossed the room and looked out the window toward the speedway. "You'd have a great view of the fireworks they shoot off after the race from here," she said, rubbing her hands up and down her bare arms.

"Are you cold?" he asked.

"A little," she said, smiling at him over her shoulder. "You must have a really high internal thermostat if you're comfortable at this temperature."

"I guess I do." It wasn't a guess. He felt as if he'd burst into flames at any moment. He shrugged out of his blazer and laid it over her shoulders before he went to the wall to adjust the temperature. "It should be warmer in a few minutes."

"Thanks." She turned away from the window and moved to the center of the room, her hands holding his blazer close against her. "Lucas, what are you going to do about Tony Winters? We're running out of time."

The anxiety he'd heard in her voice in the car had returned. Her eyes were huge, dark pools filled with questions and something more—desire. He definitely was going up in smoke and flames. There'd be nothing left of him for the fire department to find but a heap of cinders. She took two steps forward, coming so close he could smell her perfume, spicy and sexy tonight, all woman. He lowered his gaze. If he let himself go, they would both be lost.

"I have to make some calls," he said, shoving his hands into his pants pockets. "The bottled water is in the fridge below the sink. Help yourself."

She stopped in her tracks, blinking as though she had just walked into a brightly lit room. "Okay. And if you don't mind, I'll use the restroom to tidy up."

"It's right over there." He watched her walk the length of the room—in the direction of the bedroom—and almost lost his train of thought again. He spun on his heel and pulled his cell phone out of his pocket, punching in his New York precinct number with short jabs of his finger.

He hoped to hell someone was there to pick up who knew enough about the case to get word out on the street that he wanted Armando Mueller brought in for questioning without spooking the little jerk. All he needed now was his one and only link to Tony Winters going to ground in the seamy underbelly of New York City. He might not surface again for weeks, or maybe never, considering the kind of company he kept. That would be the end of it, if Winters fled the country.

The connection came to life. "Carpenter, it's Haines," he replied in response to a gruffly barked greeting on the other end of the line. "I need someone to pick up Armando Mueller, pronto." He pictured the grizzled, veteran detective, bald head shining beneath the fluorescent lights of the station house, his suit permanently wrinkled and straining over his beer belly as the older man blistered his ears with a litany of reasons why that wasn't going to happen anytime soon. Carpenter had always respected Lucas's go-it-alone attitude unlike some of the other detectives. When they did share a case, they worked well together.

"Make it happen, Lee," he interrupted without apology. "It's starting to come together down here. Winters is looking more and more like our perp. Trouble is I'm pretty sure he's getting ready to bolt to Costa Rica, and I still don't have enough to take to a judge." He listened to another grumbled response, but he could sense he'd caught the older detective's full attention. "Yeah, I'll fax you what I've got. It's a lineup of hunches at this point, nothing concrete. But if we get a positive ID out of our boy Armando it'll all come together. Mueller's the weak link in the chain, buddy, we both know that. If we lean on him hard enough, he'll cave. But we have to find him first."

Carpenter didn't give up without a fight. He rampaged on for a couple more minutes then gave a gusty sigh of surrender and promised to see what he could do. From any other man that wouldn't have been enough, but Lucas knew Carpenter wanted the Cargill case off his plate as badly as Lucas did. If Armando Mueller could be found, Carpenter would do it.

He flipped his phone shut and saw Mattie's reflection in the window. He turned around. She was standing by the couch, two glasses of sparkling water in her hands. She'd placed his blazer on the back of a chair and her bare shoulders shone pale gold in the light of the single lamp burning on the side table. He wondered what it would feel like to kiss her there, and lower on the soft curves of her chest. His mouth went dry and he had to make a physical effort to keep his hand from shaking when their fingers brushed as he accepted the glass of water.

"I couldn't help but overhear what you said."

"If I hadn't wanted you to hear I would have left the room, Mattie," he said. They were partners now, whether he had wanted it that way in the beginning or not.

She gave him a small, serious smile. "Thank you," she said softly, acknowledging the compliment, the connection. "Do you think that guy, Mueller, will really be able to identify Tony Winters?"

"He might. He's in deep with a lot of really unsavory characters. He wasn't satisfied fencing jewelry and watches, flying under the radar. He had to go for the big money and get into the drug business, a lot like Winters, I imagine. The Charlotte police don't have anything they can pin on him, but he spends a lot of time with an old high school buddy who—rumor has it," he said, unable to hide all the frustration he felt at getting the runaround, "got himself hooked up with one of the New York gangs that have been moving down the East Coast in the past couple of years."

"And Winters followed along in his wake?"

"It's not out of the realm of possibility. And it would explain a lot about why our friend Tony has the reputation but no arrests and no record. These guys throw a lot of money around. It wouldn't be the first time a cop with a lot of alimony and child support to pay looked the other way for a nice pile of cash."

"It wouldn't necessarily have to be a bad cop," she said quietly. "It could be a judge or…a politician…or someone else with enough influence to make bad things go away."

"It could be." He shrugged. "A bad cop on the take's still the most likely scenario."

"What do we do next?"

"You don't just dabble in drugs and gambling with the people Tony Winters and his pal are involved with." They had discussed this before, but they were both edgy and it helped to voice their thoughts, work through the possibilities. "These guys play for keeps. Mueller knows that. We might be able to persuade him that turning state's evidence in the Cargill case will get him a lighter sentence—and let him serve his time in a prison far, far away from the Big Apple and the guys he's in hock to."

"In other words we possess ourselves in patience."

She scowled down at her glass of sparkling water. "I hate waiting."

He reached out and took the glass from her hand, set it on the table beside his own. "So do I," he said, and took her in his arms.

She didn't protest, didn't try to hold him off. She wrapped her arms around his neck and looked straight into his eyes. Hers were dark with passion, mirroring the need in his own. "We may have to wait to bring Winters to justice," she said. "But we don't have to wait for this." She raised her mouth to his.

THIS TIME THEY DIDN'T STOP with a single kiss. She was tired of holding back the tidal wave of feelings that roared through her body, and she refused to heed the warning sirens of impending heartache, letting her desire for Lucas drown them out. She kissed him back, reveled in the touch of his mouth on her lips, her cheek, her throat.

He picked her up in his arms as if she weighed no more than a child. She tightened her grip on his neck and anchored herself to his strong, muscled chest. She didn't protest when he carried her into the bedroom of the hotel suite, didn't try to stop him when he began to stroke her, but returned the favor in kind.

They never stopped kissing as he lowered her to the bed, his hands caressing her, learning the shape of her. She followed his lead, reveling in the heat of him as he stretched full length beside her as their kisses grew more intense. She ceased to think at all, only feel. She had told Lucas she wasn't a virgin and that was true, but she had never experienced anything as intense.

The passion between them built into a tidal wave of

sensation that rocked her to the core, lifted her so high she could look down on the mountaintops and reach up to touch the stars.

MATTIE WAS NESTLED AGAINST him, her breathing soft and even. To anyone else she would appear to be asleep but he knew better. Her heartbeat was too fast; the tension in her neck and shoulders was also a giveaway. They had to talk. There was no way they could face each other come morning and pretend that what had happened between them was nothing more than stress relief, mere recreational sex. Enjoyable and mind-blowing as it had been, it had been far from casual. That was the problem, for her as much as for him, he suspected.

What were they going to do? He hadn't had a serious relationship in years. Being a cop and a lover and a husband at the same time usually didn't work. He had a lot more examples than just his parents' dysfunctional marriage to go on. He hadn't even considered the possibility of falling in love himself. Had always planned not to let it happen and so far he'd succeeded. But what he felt for Mattie was different. He wasn't ready to call it love, but he wasn't ready to turn his back on her and walk away, either.

"Mattie?" he asked softly. It was almost six. It would be light soon. He wanted to get her home before her neighbors were up and stirring and peeking from behind their curtains. "Are you awake?"

"No," she said, stretching like a cat. "I'm not. I don't want to wake up and I don't want to talk about what just happened."

He smiled into the darkness, a little of his own insecurity melting away at the defiant tone of her voice.

"What do you want to do?" he asked, running his hand over her hip. She rolled against him. "I want to go back to the same place you took me before," she whispered against his mouth, her body realigning itself to his.

"Where was that?"

"Over the rainbow, I think." She smiled as she pressed her lips to his. "I'm not sure but I'll recognize it when I get there."

LUCAS WAS ASLEEP, NOT pretending as she had been half an hour earlier. They had made love a second time even though it was against her better judgment. She couldn't seem to help herself. It was too late for lies, or even pretending. She was falling head over heels in love with a man who might as well come from a different planet, whose home and family were hundreds of miles removed from hers, whose life goals...she didn't even know.

If he opened his eyes and took her in his arms again she wouldn't resist, but she knew equally as surely that when she came back to earth this time it would be permanently, and it was going to be a very hard landing. She had never been one to look away from the reality of a situation. They needed to talk about their lovemaking, put it into perspective, figure out the next step in their relationship—she supposed it really was a relationship now, not just a ruse. Lucas Haines might be a lot of things but she didn't think he was into one-night stands any more than she was. At least she hoped he wasn't. "Lucas, are you awake?" she asked, falling into the temptation to run her fingertip across the hard lines of his collarbone and then lower to savor the rasp of his chest hair against her palm.

"I am now," he said, and reached for her again. She sucked in her breath, wishing she'd taken the precaution of putting a few more inches between them so she would have the fortitude to say no to a third bout of lovemaking. She didn't have to test her willpower. At that very moment his cell phone rang, a utilitarian sound without any bells or whistles or clever ring tones to distract from the urgency of the summons slicing through the predawn darkness.

"Damn," he said, and swung his feet over the side of the bed. Mattie took the opportunity to slide farther onto her own side and pull the covers up to her chin, fortifying her dangerously lacking self-control with a little more physical distance. "Haines," he barked into the cell.

The conversation was brief, but she didn't have to be able to hear both sides to realize what was going on. The police in New York had located Armando Mueller, but he wasn't talking. They wanted Lucas back there and pronto. Her heart sank a little. Lucas would leave Charlotte on the first plane out. There wouldn't be any time for them to come to terms with their personal situation. There surely wouldn't be time for her to pluck up her courage and tell him she loved him. That might take until the end of the world.

"I have to go," he said, flipping the phone shut. He swiveled his torso so that he could watch her face. She was ready for him. She nodded. "I assumed as much from what you said."

"Mueller's just a street punk with delusions of grandeur, but he's not stupid. He's not going to give up what he knows about Winters without trying to get something in return."

"Do you have enough evidence to keep him in jail until you get there?" He reached for his pants.

"The beat cop who brought him in found a gold pen in his belongings. It matches the description of the one Alan was carrying the night he died."

"He was trying to fence Alan's pen? The one Dean and Patsy gave him when they became partners in Cargill Motors last year?"

"I didn't know who gave it to him, but yes, they believe it's Cargill's pen."

"Did Mueller identify Tony Winters as the man who gave it to him to sell?"

"Mueller won't talk until I get there."

"Take me with you," she said, leaning toward him in her eagerness.

"I can't," he said, heading for the bathroom. "I'm sorry, Mattie, I just can't."

A cold frisson of fear skittered across her nerve endings. Not because he was refusing to take her to New York with him. She'd expected as much. The chill came from another thought that burrowed into her consciousness. Would he use those same words if she were foolish enough to ask him to stay with her for the rest of his life?

CHAPTER FOURTEEN

MATTIE FOLDED HER ARMS across her chest and stared out the window at the gorgeous autumn day. Race day. She should already be headed for the track. Traffic would be a horror if she didn't leave soon, but she remained rooted to the spot. She was so tired she could barely think. She had been awake since four.

That's when the ringing of her cell had wakened her from a fitful sleep filled with dreams of longing for a man she was afraid she would never have again. The call had been from Lucas, the first she'd spoken to him in forty-eight, long, lonely hours, and it had lived up to the heart-pounding dread that such late-night calls always engendered in her.

"Armando Mueller is dead," he said without preamble.

"But I thought he was in jail," she responded numbly, still disorientated by the shock of being awakened so abruptly.

"He was. They found him hanging in his cell."

"He committed suicide?" A shudder went through her.

"My guess is the autopsy will find he had some help. He was a liability to some very nasty characters once we picked him up again."

"Did he identify Tony Winters as the man who killed Alan?"

There was silence on the other end of the connection. She found she was holding her breath and made herself let it out and take another, then another.

"No," Lucas said after a short silence. "Damn it, he didn't."

She couldn't help it. She didn't feel any sorrow for the wasted life of Armando Mueller, only regret that he had died before he could reveal what he knew. "Now what?" she asked.

"We're back to square one." She had heard the thread of discouragement beneath the habitual even timbre of his voice. She wouldn't have been aware of it just ten days before, but she knew him now, loved him now, and the emotion came through loud and clear.

"Not quite." She wasn't going to let Alan's murder lapse into just another Big Apple cold case. She wasn't a New York cop, part of a system where the bad guys outnumbered the good guys by a factor of a hundred or more and rules and regulations hampered your every move. She was on her home ground. And she knew where Tony Winters was this very minute.

It was her turn to see what she could do with her own set of investigative skills.

"Mattie, what are you up to?" Lucas had asked.

"I won't let that man slip through our fingers. I'm convinced he killed Alan," she said, adrenaline pumping through her veins, chasing the last remnants of sleep away.

"There's nothing you can do now," he had said sharply. "It's the middle of the night."

That inarguable fact brought her up short. "What do you suggest?"

"Wait for me. I have to file the paperwork then I'll get the first flight I can wrangle a seat on."

She remembered what he had said about the woman who had ruined his father's career, the disdain with which he spoke of her. She had told him she wasn't that kind of reporter, that kind of woman. She had spoken the truth, but it was so very hard to agree, as he asked her, to wait. But she had. And so far she had kept her word.

But it was now twelve hours later, and she was still waiting. A heavy fog had descended on the Northeast as dawn neared and delayed all the flights in and out of airports not only in New York but across New England. Start time was drawing near, and any promotional appearances that Grace—and Tony Winters—were doing at the track would be winding up in preparation for the race.

Lucas was finally in the air, but he was still a couple of hours from arriving at the track. For all she knew Tony Winters was packed and ready to decamp to Costa Rica at any moment. She didn't know precisely what she could do to prevent that from happening, but she couldn't wait any longer. Despite her promise to Lucas, it was time to act.

LUCAS HAD BEEN CRAMMED into a window seat on the plane for the last five hours and he was ready to tear a hole in the fuselage with his bare hands to get his feet back on solid ground. They had sat on the runway at LaGuardia for almost two hours waiting for stacked-up aircraft from all over the East and Midwest to land before the taxiway cleared. Then there was another forty-minute wait before the plane took off. By the time they landed in Charlotte it was almost sunset. The race would be starting in less than an hour.

He punched in Mattie's number one more time. It went directly to voice mail. It had been that way for the past fifteen minutes. The only communication he'd had with her was a single text message that had popped-up in his in-box the moment the plane landed and he turned on his phone.

Since then—nothing.

He didn't like to draw attention to himself, but this time he didn't have a choice. The moment he was in the gangway, heading for the terminal, he had called the Charlotte P.D. and requested a cruiser to pick him up and take him to the track. His insides churned with nervous energy, with plain old-fashioned dread. He should have taken Mattie to New York with him. Better yet he should have chained her to the bed in his hotel room. She was fearless. She wouldn't hesitate a moment to confront the man she was now convinced had killed her friend if she concluded that there was no other way to handle the situation.

She had told him she never acted on emotion, never let her heart rule her head. He might have continued to believe that about her if they hadn't made love. He knew her better now. Beneath the surface Mattie roiled with emotions and passion. When she was sufficiently aroused, or sufficiently provoked, those emotions boiled to the surface. When that happened, she would act on instinct even if that instinct put her in danger.

His stomach turned over again. God, what would he do if something happened to her? He hadn't yet admitted to himself that he loved her, but he did know she was becoming a very, very important part of his life. He didn't think Winters was a born killer, but desperate men who had killed once would do so again if driven into a corner.

A rueful smile flickered across his lips as a picture of Mattie's stubborn, beautiful face flashed before his mind's eye. If there was one thing Steve Clayton's daughter was good at, it was driving a man into a corner—and keeping him there.

MATTIE WAS SO KEYED UP she could feel her nerve endings vibrating beneath her skin. The drive to the track had been stop-and-go as the grandstands began to fill up for the evening race. Once inside the gate, she parked her car in a VIP lot, thankful for the parking pass that gave her the privilege. She wished Lucas was with her, but he wasn't. She had promised him she would keep a low profile, and she intended to, but she simply had to be here, doing her best to keep an unobtrusive eye on Tony Winters.

The first place she intended to look was the media center. She might get lucky and find someone who had seen Grace, or even a printed handout of her schedule for the day. If Mattie struck out there, she would head for the VIP suites and start snooping around. If necessary she would enlist her father's aid in tracking down Grace and her brother-in-law.

Mattie passed through track security and started along the row of titanic, gaudily painted haulers that were the nerve centers of the race teams at the track. She thought she heard someone call her name and turned to find she was being hailed by a woman dressed in jeans and sturdy—NASCAR-mandated—shoes, a brown Turn-Rite tools ball cap on her head and a clipboard in her hand. "Mattie, wait up a moment," Sophia Murphy called over the heads of a pair of Trey Sanford's crew members. "What luck I ran into you. I've got something I want to tell you."

"Sophia? I thought you'd be down on pit road by now. It's almost time for the driver introductions." NASCAR drivers could be a superstitious lot and so could their wives. Sophia never missed walking her husband to his car before a race.

"I'm heading there right now but I'm so glad I ran into you," her friend repeated. "I didn't want to have to tell you this over the phone."

"You sound very conspiratorial."

Sophia's smile disappeared. She pulled Mattie into the small space between two of the haulers. Mattie marveled, as she always did, how it was possible to park them so closely together with almost laser-straight precision. "I have news about Tony Winters."

"What kind of information?" Mattie demanded. The cars were silent for the moment, the huge engines at rest as the garage crews readied them to be rolled out onto the track, but the shouts of team members calling to one another, the noise from tens of thousands of fans already in their seats, the amplified voices of the public address announcers and background music from half a dozen sources made it impossible to speak in anything but a half shout.

"Justin's chief mechanic's sister is married to the car chief at Matheson," Sophia began, describing one of the numerous intertwining relationships between the race teams. "A couple of guys went back to the shop to get some tools they forgot to load."

"And..." Mattie prompted, wondering exactly where Sophia was taking the conversation. Since they were racing in Concord, close by many of the race teams' headquarters, it wasn't an unusual occurrence to send crew members back to the shop.

"And they found a bunch of suits there. At Matheson. Today. On a Saturday. Pencil pushers, the guys described them." Sophia reached out and squeezed Mattie's hand. "Auditor types."

Mattie shivered, racing to her own conclusion. "Looking for irregularities in the books."

"Yes, exactly." Sophia nodded excitedly. "Tony Winters was an accountant for the team for a while. There have been rumors circulating ever since he 'quit' working there that Chad Matheson caught him skimming money," she said, quotation marks hovering in her voice. "Remember we talked about Tony that night you brought Lucas to the farm."

"I remember," Mattie said grimly.

"Chad Matheson is a good guy, but he won't let someone take advantage of him or get away with a crime. I think he's having his books audited because Tony Winters stole a lot more money from him than he first thought. A lot more money than he could afford to ignore," Sophia finished triumphantly.

"Sophia, have you told anyone else what you just told me?" Mattie leaned slightly closer although they were as private as they could be in the midst of the prerace hoopla. Mattie replayed her conversation with Winters in the VIP elevator. He was planning on leaving the country on "vacation," she recalled, adding her own mental quotation marks. Costa Rica. That's where he'd be heading when he heard the gossip Sophia had just repeated to her. And he would hear it, there was no question of that. "Anyone at all?"

Sophia shook her head, sending the ponytail she'd pulled through the back of her cap bobbing emphatically. "No one. I just heard it myself, but that doesn't mean it won't be all over the race track by the time Justin takes his victory lap. I can't believe I was lucky enough to find you so soon."

"I need to keep my eye on Tony Winters until I can contact Lucas," Mattie said. "Do you have any idea where Winters is?" *If he was even at the race track.* There was no guarantee he was still on the grounds.

"I do. He's at the media center. With Grace and her niece Sadie." Sophia's face paled. "And Nana. Sadie's interviewing them for a school report. Women in NASCAR." She gripped Mattie's hand tighter. "I'll come with you." Sophia was as eager to find Alan's killer as Mattie was, but that didn't mean Mattie intended to let her friend put herself in harm's way.

"No," Mattie said. "It will be better if I'm alone. I'm in and out of the media center all the time. He might get spooked if we show up together."

"But Nana...and Sadie."

"Are both perfectly safe in the media center," Mattie assured her. "It's time for the opening ceremonies. You need to be there to walk Justin to his car." As though to back up her words, the loudspeakers blared forth the information that opening ceremonies would begin in five minutes. "Go," she said, giving Sophia a little push.

"I'll go," Sophia said reluctantly. "But be careful, Mattie," she urged, already beginning to walk away. "Don't do anything foolish. Wait for Lucas. He's the pro."

"I hope I can," Mattie said under her breath, and turned her steps toward the media center where her unsuspecting—she hoped—quarry awaited.

SOMEONE IN THE CHARLOTTE P.D. had made a call, Lucas realized, passing along information on the outsider in their midst. It was okay; he would have done the same if the situation was reversed. An armed security guard beckoned him through a small, inconspicuous door in the main building that led into a starkly utilitarian command room. A tall, black man rose from a chair in front of a bank of monitors. He had the look of ex-military, Special Forces, probably. "Welcome to my lair, Detective."

Lucas held out his hand. "Lucas Haines, NYPD," he said, showing the man his badge.

"Josiah Harris, track security," the older man replied, waving off the proffered credentials. "We understand you have reason to believe there might be a fugitive on race track property."

"We have a subject of interest in the Alan Cargill murder that I'd like to question," Lucas said. "He's credentialed, not just a fan. You have some way of tracking him down for me?"

"Busy night," Harris said cryptically, giving Lucas a long, hard look. "I'm doing some tracking of my own. An embezzler. Do you have a name for your person of interest?"

"Winters," Lucas said, the hair on the back of his neck rising as he processed the security officer's words. "His name is Tony Winters."

"Tony Winters. Now isn't that a coincidence." Chief Harris propped one hip on the counter fronting a bank of monitors that took in most of the race track operations. "That's the same guy I'm looking for. Seems he was skimming money off the top at the race team he was working for. Now you're tellin' me he's your prime suspect in the Alan Cargill murder?"

"Yes, but when I left New York this morning I had no information that he was wanted for any crimes in Concord."

"Matheson Racing filed a complaint a few hours ago. Seems Chad Matheson hired an auditor and found there was substantially more money missing from his accounts than Winters had 'fessed up to skimming when he fired him."

"I see," Lucas said, choosing his words carefully. "Does that mean you're pulling rank on me?"

"It is my turf," Harris said mildly.

"Murder trumps embezzlement every time," Lucas said. He studied his companion for a brace of heartbeats. Should he step back and let Harris take the point? He didn't want Winters put on his guard by a score of track security on a public manhunt, but neither did he want him sashaying out of the main gate and flying off into the Costa Rican sunset.

Harris made his decision for him. "I know what you're thinking. Glorified rent-a-cops poking their noses in every doorway. Skittish perp gets the heebie-jeebies and makes himself scarce. That's not how I run my operation, Haines." He folded his arms across his chest. "I've got damned good people and we keep a close eye on everything that goes on here. Hell, do you know the seating capacity of this place? We've got a fair-size city of fans milling around out there. Unless you can pinpoint our perp right now, you're going to need help finding him. Charlotte P.D. wants you to be in the lead on this one and Concord signed off, too. That leaves little ol' me for you to reckon with." He stood up, towering over Lucas by a good three inches. "What do you want me to do?"

"I'll take all the help I can get," Lucas said. "Here's what I have. A friend got word to me not too long ago that Winters had been spotted in the media center. He might not be there anymore." That second text message from Mattie had been cryptic, saying only that Tony might be spooked by activity at Matheson Racing and she was going to look for him at the track media center. Lucas owed the Concord cops one for getting him to the track so fast with race night traffic as heavy as it was, but the message was still almost forty minutes old.

Harris beckoned one of his minions. "Go with Morrissey here. He knows how to keep a low profile,"

A man stepped out of the shadows of the crowded room, small, compactly built, tough looking. He nodded to Lucas, hooked his thumbs into his utility belt and waited for instructions.

The Charlotte P.D. officer that had driven Lucas in from the airport, nodded, also. "We'll be ready on the outside if he leaves the property." He touched his finger to the brim of his hat and headed back to his cruiser, the guard who had escorted Lucas through the gate and into the room, a step behind. Harris motioned to Lucas to come closer. He consulted his monitors again.

"Grace Winters was here most of the day doing some kind of promo stuff for a cookbook, or a TV show, maybe both. According to the log, she finished her last shoot, in the infield camping area, about an hour ago. We don't have any more information on her. She and Tony might have gone to the media center like you said. I can make a call and find out."

"I don't want him spooked," Lucas said tightly.

Harris didn't bother to answer, just grunted and checked another bank of monitors as though Grace and her brother-in-law might turn up on one of them. He picked up a handset, spoke a few curt sentences and waited. "Yeah, thanks. If he comes back, I want to know before the door swings shut on his backside. Understood?" He swiveled to face Lucas.

"Winters and his sister-in-law were in the media center earlier, like you said. Been gone fifteen minutes or so. Left with Juliana Grosso, of all the damned people, and another woman my man didn't recognize."

Lucas had the terrible suspicion that he would recognize the woman instantly. But Juliana Grosso was an unexpected complication. What was she doing with them?

"Since they've all got hard cards they could be anywhere on the grounds. I'll get the word out to my guys to be on the lookout, but we're spread pretty thin tonight. You've got as good a chance finding them on your own. I'll get you a Club Car." He smiled, his mouth stretching into a grin that reminded Lucas of a Great White just before its jaws clamped down on a hapless sea lion. "It's one of ours. May not hit 160 on the backstretch but you can outrun any cart on the property."

Lucas held out his hand again. "Thanks for the help. I'll keep you in the loop."

"Don't worry. I'll be in the loop," Harris said. "If you let him slip through your fingers, you can be damned sure I won't."

"Understood," Lucas replied.

"I hope you get him. Alan Cargill was well respected around these parts."

"I intend to." Finding Winters was one thing. Getting

him to confess was something else. "And, Chief," he said, letting his personal anxiety for Mattie's safety get the better of him. "There's one other person I'd like your men to keep a lookout for."

"Who's that?"

"Mattie Clayton."

"Steve Clayton's daughter? Is that by any chance the woman my guy didn't recognize?"

"I think it might be."

"She's out there, looking for Winters on her own?"

"It's a good possibility."

Harris whistled through his teeth. "Great, that's all I need, an amateur sleuth on the trail of a possible murder suspect in the middle of a race. Anything else you forgot to tell me that I might want to know?"

"No," Lucas said grimly. "But you can tell me something. Since we came up empty at the media center, give me your best guess where the three of them might be."

CHAPTER FIFTEEN

MATTIE HAD NO TROUBLE entering the track media center. The guard at the entrance let her through after a quick glance at her credentials. The noise level inside the building was almost as high a decibel as it was outside. The room was half-full of men, and a few women, seated at rows of curved desks equipped with Internet hookups and telephones, all with a view of a quartet of big-screen TVs tuned to different areas of the race track itself, the pits and the garage area. Most of the print and electronic reporters were watching the race from their desks, taking in all of the action from a central location instead of from the more limited view even the best seats in the grandstand provided. Most of the TV crews were out on the track, doing their thing.

She waved greetings to a half dozen familiar faces, smiling as though she were only there to say hello, while her mind formed and discarded strategies to let Lucas know where she was and what she was doing. She'd texted him before heading to the media center, and she now had her cell phone in her hand ready to punch in his number on speed dial when a door to a small interview room opened and Grace, Tony Winters and Nana emerged. Ethan's little girl was nowhere to be seen. Mattie was glad of that, one less complication to deal with. She dropped the cell phone back into her jacket pocket. Maybe this detective gig wasn't as difficult as she had thought.

"Why, how nice, it's Mattie," Juliana sang out, bracelets jingling as she beckoned Mattie closer. "What are you doing here? Ferreting out high crimes and misdemeanors in stock car racing?" she asked with a wink.

"Just touching base, Nana," Mattie said, giving the old woman's hand a quick squeeze. "Hello, Grace. Hello, Tony," she said, holding on to her smile with an effort.

"Grace and Tony and I just finished an interview with Ethan's little girl," Nana explained. "She's doing a paper on women in NASCAR and she was kind enough to include me. Such a sweet child. Cassie collected her a few minutes ago. We're on our way to the motor home to have a drink with Milo. And now, you must come, too. You know how Milo loves to share a glass of wine with a pretty girl." She turned to Grace and patted her cheek. "And now he will have two. Doesn't that sound like a good idea, Mattie, dear?"

"It…it sounds wonderful, Nana. Thanks for the invitation." She caught Tony Winters's quick scowl from the corner of her eye. He didn't think it was a good idea for her to tag along, that was for sure.

The old lady's eyes flared with satisfaction. "Excellent. I have a Club Car waiting outside. Tony, you will do an old lady a favor and drive, won't you?"

"I'm afraid I have to beg off, Mrs. Grosso. There are things I have to do—"

"Nonsense." Juliana dismissed his excuse with another wave of her hand. "All that will wait. Come, Grace. A glass of wine will do you good. You look worn to the bone."

"I am, Nana," Grace confessed. "It has been a very, very long day."

"See, Tony, Grace needs a chance to unwind a bit before you take her home to her children." She shooed Tony and Mattie ahead of her toward the entrance to the building, making it impossible for Mattie to stop and text Lucas their whereabouts.

Nana's field marshaling didn't have the same effect on Tony Winters's communications, though. His cell beeped, signaling the arrival of a message. He muttered an excuse and walked a couple of feet away from the group as Nana and Grace arranged themselves in the backseat of the Club Car, leaving Mattie to ride shotgun. But the man who slid onto the seat beside her a few moments later was not the same one who had walked through the media center doorway less than two minutes earlier. His face was ashen, his mouth drawn into a straight, hard line. His hands shook as he turned the key in the ignition. When he swiveled his head to check for traffic behind him before backing the cart onto the narrow roadway leading out of the infield, Mattie's heart jumped into her throat.

He looked as if he had seen a ghost. Whatever he'd learned, it hadn't been good news. She didn't have to be a psychic to figure out what information he'd received. Someone—a buddy from the shop, another accountant, maybe even a crooked cop—had tipped him off to the activity at Matheson Racing. Tony Winters was a hunted man and he knew it.

And then his eyes met hers. They were filled with fear and anger, and something more, a flare of hope and a kind of calculating challenge, directed solely at her. His look heightened her state of alert. But as quickly as it came the madness disappeared, leaving her feeling slightly disoriented and more than a little paranoid.

"Too loud to hear yourself think," he yelled with a smile as forty-three race cars thundered down the frontstretch.

"Yes." She nodded and pushed her hand into the pocket of her jacket, folding her fingers around her cell phone and the equally small digital recorder she always kept with her, wishing for the first time in her life that one of them was a weapon instead.

Tony headed the cart toward the VIP lot where most of the drivers' and some of the crew chiefs' motor homes were parked. Other than the guard at the gate, they saw no one Mattie could appeal to for help, and the guard waved them through with a respectful finger to the brim of his cap when he recognized Juliana in the backseat. They pulled up in front of one of the high-end motor homes the Grossos were occupying for the weekend. Even though most of the NASCAR teams were based in Charlotte and nearby towns, they still brought their motor homes to the track to avoid spending hours in traffic, and to have someplace private to spend what little leisure time they had.

Mattie felt a moment of real panic as the Club Car came to a halt, but she refused to acknowledge it. The motor homes on either side of Milo and Juliana's were dark and silent, as were the ones directly across the graveled roadway. She was on her own. It didn't take her a moment to decide she would do everything she could to keep Tony Winters in sight until she could alert Lucas to their whereabouts. It wasn't much of a plan, but it was the only one she could come up with on such short notice.

"We're here," Juliana announced. "Come inside."

Grace complied with Juliana's request and exited

the cart at the same time her hostess did. Mattie fiddled with the shoulder strap of her small leather bag, watching as Tony's hand hovered over the gearshift as though he might be contemplating making a run for it. If he did, she would have to find some way to stop him. Once more she closed her hand around the cell phone in her pocket. If she punched him in the face while she had it in her hand, it would surely do enough damage to slow him down for a short period of time. Time enough to get Juliana and Grace to safety and to call Lucas or 9-1-1.

Tony shifted his gaze to hers. She hoped nothing of what she was thinking had imprinted itself on her expression. She smiled, and it felt as if she'd managed to make it a good one. Once more that quick flash of cunning and calculation lit Tony's eyes then disappeared. Once more he smiled, overfriendly and ingratiating. All she could do now was behave as if she hadn't a suspicion in the world that Tony was a wanted man, an embezzler, a coldblooded murderer. She prayed she was a good enough actor to bring it off.

LUCAS ARRIVED AT STEVE Clayton's suite exactly five minutes after he left the media center. No one there had known where Grace Winters and the others had gone, although one print reporter coming out of the men's room volunteered that he had heard Juliana talking about inviting the others somewhere. He didn't remember where, but everyone in NASCAR knew Juliana Grosso held court in the VIP suites at every race she attended. It was the only lead he had. Lucas followed it.

Steve Clayton crossed the crowded suite the moment he spotted Lucas standing in the doorway. The noise of the race track several stories below was slightly less ear-shattering in the rarified atmosphere of the VIP suites, but the decibel level was still high enough to make normal speech difficult. "Have you seen Mattie in the last fifteen minutes or so?" Lucas asked without preamble.

"She hasn't been here this evening," Steve said, placing his arm around his wife's shoulder as she excused herself from a small knot of people to join them. She was wearing some kind of silky gray dress and jacket, upscale casual, as were all their other guests, making Lucas aware, momentarily, of his own rumpled and travel-stained appearance.

"We thought she would have joined us by now. Unless she's in another suite," Sarah offered. "Or somewhere else in the building."

"Or out of it," Lucas said grimly, remembering the sea of humanity he'd wended his way through to get where he was. "She was seen leaving the media center with Juliana Grosso and Grace Winters and Grace's brother-in-law."

"Did I hear my grandmother's name mentioned?" Dean Grosso moved away from the bar and came to a halt directly in front of Lucas. "Is something wrong?"

"There might be. Grace and Juliana were with Tony Winters. Mattie went looking for him."

"Went looking for Winters? Why?" Steve demanded. Lucas sifted through the facts, deciding how much information to give Mattie's father. "She heard a rumor that Matheson Racing was getting ready to file charges against Winters for embezzlement."

"Are the rumors true?" Sarah asked, her hand at her throat.

"Yes."

"Oh, dear. Steve?" She looked up at her husband. His expression was grim as he took in the implications of Lucas's revelation.

"Mattie wouldn't do anything foolish. She wouldn't take risks with Juliana around."

"I hope not," Lucas said, before he could stop himself. Steve Clayton's frown deepened, but it was Dean Grosso who spoke next.

"If they're still all together and not in one of the other suites, they're probably headed back to the motor home. Milo's there. His arthritis is acting up so he didn't feel like watching Kent race from the war wagon. I can give Nana a call."

"No. I don't want Winters to get any suspicions we're onto him."

"It might be too late," Dean said, his brows pulled together in a frown. "If Mattie's heard rumors then likely so have a lot of other people."

The same thought had already occurred to Lucas. "I have a cart and driver outside," he said, making up his mind. He didn't need more civilians dogging his heels, but if he didn't give these two alpha males something to do they wouldn't get more than two feet away from him for the rest of the night. "You two check out the suites. This is your territory, not mine. If there's one thing I've learned the past months it's that NASCAR people won't open up to a NYPD detective like they will one of their own. If you spot them, don't try anything heroic. Get security ASAP. Understand?"

Steve and Dean exchanged looks. "Agreed. Is your driver track security?" Steve asked.

"Yes."

"He'll get you through the checkpoints in the VIP

area and show you where Milo's motor home is parked. If he doesn't know which one it is, tell him its right next to mine," Dean said.

"If we don't find Mattie and Juliana up here, we'll be right behind you," Steve added.

Lucas didn't waste his breath arguing with them. He'd be doing the same thing if their roles were reversed.

"WE CAN ONLY STAY A MINUTE or two, Nana," Grace said gently, casting an apologetic glance at her brother-in-law. "Tony and I need to leave the track while the traffic is light. I want to get home to my children, and Tony has last-minute packing to do before his trip to Costa Rica tomorrow."

That would account for some of Tony's recent panic, Mattie surmised. He might be able to stay out of custody if he went to ground nearby, but the police would surely be watching the airports and that would put paid to his plans to leave the country and disappear.

"Excellent." Juliana mounted the steps of the motor home and opened the door. "A small glass of wine for everyone, and maybe just a bite to eat. I have a wonderful new artichoke dip I whipped up this afternoon. Mattie, why don't you try to get that handsome detective of yours on your cell. Invite him to join us. Where is he by the way?"

"Oh, he's around," she said, fervently wishing she was right. "I'll do just that." Bless Juliana. The garrulous old lady had given her the opening she needed.

"No, you won't," Tony said in her ear, his voice a quiet rasp. "No calls to Detective Haines." He yanked the cell phone from her hand before she could whisk it out of his reach and dropped it into his jacket pocket.

"What in the world," she said, not having to fake the shock and outrage in her voice at all. "Give me my phone back."

"When we're ready to leave," he said, his smile turning into a death's head grimace. The acrid scent of sweat and fear assaulted Mattie's nostrils. "We're leaving here together."

"You can't be serious," Mattie hissed back at him. Juliana and Grace were just inside the entrance to the motor home, greeting Milo, their backs to them for the moment.

"On the contrary, I'm dead serious. You know, don't you? You know about the audit that damned Matheson had run on his books. You know he's filed a complaint against me. That there's a warrant out for my arrest."

It wasn't going to do any good to lie, Mattie decided. He wouldn't believe her anyway. Tony kept glancing into the shadows as though he suspected they had been followed. She wondered if he'd also heard about Armando Mueller's death? If he hadn't, she certainly wasn't going to tell him. He was desperate enough.

"I heard a rumor," Mattie said. "But I doubt the others have. Don't be a fool. Go inside. Make an excuse to leave. Disappear. I'll keep my mouth shut. It will take Grace and the Grossos a while to figure it out. Long enough for you to get away." She wanted this man brought to justice for her friend's death but not at the risk of the others.

"Oh, no, you don't. That little scenario might work if you were someone else, Mattie Clayton. Anyone else. But you're not. I'm going to Costa Rica tonight just like I planned. The only difference is you're going, too. Both of us. Together. In your father's plane." He took his hand out of his pocket. He wasn't holding her cell phone any longer but a small revolver. "You make some excuse to my sister-in-law and that damned old biddy and her husband," he said hoarsely. "And make it a good one. We don't have much time."

"Tony?" Grace peered out of the open doorway of the motor home. "What's going on out here?"

He flicked his wrist. "Talk," he growled.

A glimmer of moonlight, or a reflection from the lights inside the motor home must have outlined the revolver. Before Mattie could say anything Grace spoke up. "My Lord, is that a gun?"

"Damn it." Tony looked over his shoulder again. "Get inside," he ordered, prodding Mattie with the weapon. They climbed the stairs. Grace took a couple of steps backward into the main salon, her eyes wide and disbelieving. Tony gave Mattie a shove and slammed the door behind them.

"What the hell is going on?" Milo uncoiled himself from the depths of a big, overstuffed recliner. He was a small man, diminished physically by his ninety-plus years, but his voice still held a whiplash of authority. All heads turned in his direction. Tony jumped and the gun wavered for a moment before he steadied it again. He was a man on the thin edge of desperation, and all the more dangerous because of it.

"Stay put," he ordered, waving the gun in Milo's direction.

Milo took a tottering step forward. "Put that gun away before you hurt someone, you damned fool."

"Shut up, Granddad." Tony gave Milo a shove that sent him staggering back a step.

"Why you—"

"Milo!" Juliana rushed to her husband's side to steady him. He put his arm around her shoulders and held her close to his side.

"Tony, my God, what are you doing? This is madness. These people are our friends." Grace's voice trembled. She sounded as if she were trapped in the middle of a waking nightmare.

"I don't have a choice, Grace," he said bleakly, his expression half pleading, half defiant. "Chad Matheson turned me in for embezzlement. I have to get out of the country. Tonight."

"But you told me that was a misunderstanding. That you'd made some mistakes, but you corrected them."

"He lied," Mattie said between clenched teeth. "Now he thinks he can kidnap me and hijack my father's plane to fly him to Costa Rica."

Grace looked at Mattie then back to her brother-in-law. "Tony, no. Don't even think of such a thing," she pleaded. "Embezzlement is one thing. But kidnapping…" Grace shook her head, at a loss for words. "We'll get you a lawyer. I'll loan you the money to pay back Chad Matheson. Just let Mattie go."

"It's too late, Grace," Tony grated out. "It's way too late for that."

A look of dawning horror slipped across Grace's features. "Tony, what are you saying?"

"Nothing, Grace. Nothing. This whole thing's making me crazy. Don't pay any attention. I've got to go now." He motioned at Mattie with the gun. "I promise I won't hurt her." The dark look he gave her promised no such thing.

"Tony, answer me. What could be more terrible than

kidnapping? There's only one thing." She covered her face with her hands. "Murder?"

"Grace, don't say anything else. Not in front of witnesses. Not in front of her." He waved the gun in Mattie's face. "She's been nosing around too much lately. Showing up at all the parties and the book promotions. Her and that damned New York cop. Everything was fine until you two teamed up. You started the ball rolling, started people thinking about Alan's murder again just like you probably got Matheson thinking about the money. You've even got my sister-in-law believing I'm a murderer."

"Tony, please swear to me you didn't kill anyone." Grace's voice dropped to a whisper. "Swear to me."

"My God, Grace. Don't say anything else," he pleaded, almost begging. "Just don't say anything else."

"Did you kill Alan Cargill?" Mattie demanded, unable to hold back the question. "Did you kill my friend?" She was appalled to hear the words come out of her mouth. She might have goaded Tony into doing something rash and terrible. Lucas would never forgive her for acting on impulse this way. She might never forgive herself.

"Shut up, bitch," he hissed. "Get your hands out of your pockets and keep them where I can see them or I'll pop you right now." Sick at heart, Mattie did as she was told, but not before she flipped the switch on the tiny recorder. She only hoped it would pick up what was being said through the fabric of her jacket.

"Tony, no!" Grace moved to shield Mattie, but Tony ordered her back.

"Get away from her. I don't want to shoot anyone but I will if I have to."

"Tony, this is madness."

"I'm in deep with guys who play for keeps. I needed money bad. Matheson was already suspicious of me. I'd been skimming from the team to keep their muscle off my back. I thought Cargill might loan me the money if I told him they'd threatened to come after you next. The bastard turned me down flat. Said he didn't believe me, threatened to call the police then and there. I did it for you, Grace."

"For me? You killed Alan for *me?*"

"It was an accident," he yelled, then he took a deep breath as though trying to regain control. "If he'd just given me the money like I asked, it wouldn't have happened. But it's too late now to go back and make things right."

"I don't understand," Grace said, half sobbing.

"Enough talk. Sit down on the couch, Grace. All of you sit down! I don't want you in the line of fire if Miss Genius Reporter here tries anything heroic."

Milo lowered himself stiffly onto the arm of the couch, tugging Juliana down beside him. Mattie gave Grace a little push in the same direction. Grace sat. Mattie didn't.

The damage was done. She couldn't recall her rash question so now all she could do was keep Tony where he was, keep him talking and hope Lucas tracked them down—in time. "Tony killed Alan, Grace," Mattie reaffirmed quietly.

Grace's expression was disbelieving. "No. That's not true. It's not possible." Juliana reached over and took Grace's hand between her own.

"I'm afraid it is true," Mattie said with real remorse.

"You and that detective just couldn't leave well

enough alone, could you?" Tony turned the gun in Mattie's direction again.

Mattie wasn't sure what to do next. The Grosso motor home was large and roomy, but five adults in one confined area left little space to maneuver, and there was nothing she could do against a gun. She tried reasoning with Tony, although she didn't have much hope it would work. "Don't you think you owe Grace an explanation? She's the one that will have to face your family. Your mother."

Tony winced and the gun barrel lowered for a second or two before steadying. Mattie tensed but the moment of weakness passed. His expression hardened and stayed that way. "It was an accident, I tell you. I only wanted to ask Alan for a loan."

"I would have loaned you the money, Tony, I told you that."

"I think you'll find you already have, Grace," Mattie said.

Recognition dawned in Grace's eyes. "You've been stealing from the company, too?"

"I didn't have any choice!" Tony all but whined. "Matheson was breathing down my neck and I've...I've got other debts. I'll pay you back, Gracie, I promise."

"How?" she asked, bewildered. "You'll be in jail."

"I'll be in Costa Rica. I'll figure out a way to make money down there. I'll pay you back, I swear, I will."

"I don't want your money," Grace said with awful finality.

True panic flared behind Tony's hunted expression. "The damned old man told me to go to hell. Said I was a worthless leech and the whole family would be better off if I was in jail. I just...snapped. I couldn't take it any longer. I didn't have a gun on me, but I had a knife. I've been carrying one for months now."

"Who are you talking about?"

"The drug dealers he's been hooked up with," Mattie explained quietly, although it took all her willpower to keep her voice from shaking. "Tony's right. The guys he's in hock to play for keeps."

"Twelve more hours that's all I needed. Your damned cop boyfriend had to round up Armando and haul him to jail. Then those damn auditors blew my plans right out of the sky. I'll never get through airport security now without an insurance policy. You and your dad's jet." His lips curled in a sneer. "Simple and foolproof."

Grace paid little attention to his boasting. "Why did you kill Alan? He wouldn't really have turned you in. You're one of us. You're Todd's brother. He thought the world of Todd."

"I'm telling you for the last time I only meant to scare him into keeping his mouth shut. The bastard jumped me." He was pleading with her to believe him.

"You stabbed him. You killed him in cold blood." Grace put her hands to her cheeks. Tears streaked her face, but it was the look of utter loathing she turned on her brother-in-law that seemed to be the last straw.

"It was an accident I keep telling you," he screamed out of control. "He came at me. I waved the knife and he made a grab for it, crazy old coot. He tripped, or slipped, or something...." His voice broke. "There was nothing I could do."

Grace was crying openly now, her hands shielding her face. Tony stared at her, utterly dejected. Mattie had trouble not looking away from the naked misery in his expression, but she dared not lower her guard, even for a moment. Juliana put her arms around Grace and rocked her as though she were a baby.

"I've got to get out of here," Tony said, tearing his eyes away from his brother's widow. "That damned cop will be here sooner or later."

"There's no place for you to go, Tony. The police will never let my father's plane take off. Don't get yourself in deeper than you already have."

"Shut up, bitch." He jerked her to his side. The gun was so close Mattie could reach out and touch the barrel. "We're leaving. Like I said, you're my ticket out of Charlotte and out of the country."

He pulled Mattie's cell phone out of his pocket. "Call your dad," he commanded. "Get him on the line and tell him to fire up that jet of his. Explain to him that if he does exactly what I tell him he'll get you and his expensive bird back safe and sound. Otherwise..." He didn't finish the sentence just lifted the gun so that it pointed right between her eyes. He pantomimed pulling the trigger. "Boom. You'll never live to see that little brother or sister you've got coming."

CHAPTER SIXTEEN

LUCAS COULD SEE MOST OF the interior of the motor home through the half-open blinds as he stood hidden in the shadows just outside the door. Milo was seated on the edge of the couch arm, Juliana and Grace side by side next to him. Tony Winters and Mattie were just to his left. Winters was holding a gun pointed directly at her head. Winters had moved up in the world of violence, it seemed. Now he was carrying a gun instead of a switchblade, probably a wise precaution for a man with both the police and a gang of ruthless drug dealers on his tail. It was easier to kill a man with a gun.

Easier still to shoot a defenseless woman.

Lucas called on his dozen years of military and law enforcement discipline to put aside the fact that the woman staring down the barrel of the Saturday Night Special in Winters's hands was Mattie—his Mattie—and concentrated on how he was going to take the other man down without harming any of the occupants of the motor home.

He waved off the track security guard who had driven him to within a hundred feet of the Grosso motor home. Lucas gave a short, sharp hand signal and the man backed off a dozen yards and began radioing information to his boss. Harris would see to it the VIP lot was sealed off. A second guard, who had joined them at the lot entrance, would make sure no unsuspecting driver's wife or children came barreling down the row of motor homes, straight into the middle of this whole damned mess.

Winters was gesturing Mattie toward the door. Lucas leveled the barrel of his weapon, steadying it in cradled hands. He could pick off Winters where he stood but he'd have a better line of fire when Winters exited the motor home. Lucas melted a step farther into the darkness beneath the rolled-out awning. He could hear the sound of an electric cart coming in their direction but ignored it. He needed to concentrate his full attention on Winters, watching his target's eyes as he moved around the salon, reading his body language, anticipating his next move.

"Tony, for the last time, don't do this," Grace pleaded.

Lucas lifted his head a few inches to get a better look at the interior of the motor home. Milo was still perched on the arm of the couch, looking like a fierce old bird of prey, his knotted hands fisted on his thighs. Juliana had shifted position slightly, wrapping her arms comfortingly around Grace. Mattie stood alone, her stance defiant, but he knew her well enough now to sense the underlying fear she was hiding so well.

"Keep quiet, Grace," Winters returned. He had a cell phone to his ear. He flipped it shut with a mumbled curse. "No damned reception in this high-end tin can," he muttered. "C'mon. You can call your old man once we get outside."

When Mattie didn't move quickly enough, he reached out and jerked her to his side, pushing the barrel of the gun against her cheek as he wrapped his free arm around her throat. "If any one of you moves so much as an inch from where you're sitting, I'll kill her. Do you understand?"

"We understand, you bastard," Milo answered for the women.

"Open the door," he ordered Mattie. "Move."

"Mattie, don't go." Grace began to cry. "You can't trust him to keep his word."

"It's all right, Grace," Mattie said. "I'll be fine. He needs me."

He heard Mattie give a small grunt of pain as Winters pressed the gun painfully against her temple. Lucas fought his own incipient panic and managed to lock down his emotions and remain detached from the fear for Mattie that scoured his heart. The door opened; light from the salon spilled down the steps. Lucas moved back another step away from the window, ready, if need be, to put a bullet in Winters's brain.

The hydraulically operated steps lowered automatically as the door opened. Mattie emerged first, held at an awkward angle against Tony's side. She looked directly at Lucas. He saw her eyes widen as she glimpsed him in the shadows. Winters was a step above and behind her, still looking back into the interior at his other hostages.

Mattie stopped in her tracks, the last thing Lucas wanted her to do. Keep moving, he yelled in his head but she couldn't hear him. Winters, at the end of his tether, screamed at Mattie to get moving. Lucas held his position, waiting for an opening, however small, to take him down.

His finger tightened on the trigger as a flurry of

movement from within the motor home flickered into focus at the edge of his vision. He held his fire. A fraction of a second, a heartbeat later, Winters let out a startled yell and pitched forward. Mattie fell too, wrenching herself free of Tony's stranglehold as they both tumbled headlong down the steps. The force of the fall propelled her directly into Lucas's arms.

He caught her with one hand and propped her up against the side of the motor home, his eyes never leaving Winters's sprawled form. He could see the security guards already closing in, but he was closest and got there first. Before Tony could struggle to his feet, Lucas kicked the gun out of his hand, hearing the satisfying snap of breaking bones. Winters screamed in agony and rolled into a fetal position, cradling his broken wrist.

"Go ahead, shoot him," Milo yelled from the top of the steps. "I'll swear it was self-defense."

"He pushed me," Winters moaned. "The old bastard pushed me down the steps."

"I may be old but I can still move when I have to, you sniveling coward. Get this piece of human refuse out of here," Milo ordered one of the track guards. "Worthless trash." He waved his fist at the prone man. "And don't call me Granddad."

Lucas reached down and hauled Winters to his feet. He screamed in pain. "You broke my wrist. I'll sue you for police brutality. I'll have your badge," he blustered, tears running down his face.

Lucas ignored the impotent threat. "You're under arrest for the murder of Alan Cargill and the attempted abduction of Mattie Clayton. Oh, yeah, and the embezzlement of fifty thousand dollars from Matheson Racing. If I were you, I'd keep my mouth shut until I had a lawyer."

"It doesn't matter if he ever opens his mouth again," Mattie said, limping forward. Her face was white with pain but she managed a shaky smile. "I've got it all here." She reached into her pocket and pulled out a small digital recorder, waving it triumphantly in her erstwhile captor's face.

Lucas turned his head and stared at her. There was a bruise on the side of her cheek and a trickle of blood where the grip of the gun had abraded her skin. A surge of rage swept through him, but he kept it tightly leashed. This worthless piece of flesh and blood had dared to terrorize…the woman he loved. The realization stopped him in his tracks. *The woman he loved.* Was that really what he felt for Mattie?

He'd never been in love, never experienced such an emotional rollercoaster as he was on right now. His insides churned with the conflicting desires to take her in his arms, or to shake her until her teeth rattled. He thrust Winters into the hands of the other two guards. "He's all yours. Get him out of here. Tell your boss I'll head downtown to file the paperwork as soon as I make sure everyone's okay here." He shoved his weapon back into the shoulder holster before anyone noticed how badly he was shaking.

All he wanted now was to carry Mattie off somewhere and make love to her again until the terror that had stalked him all day long was burned away by desire and release. But instead of pulling her into his arms and telling her he loved her, his fear and anger got the better of him. "What the hell kind of stunt was that? Don't you know you could have gotten yourself killed? Gotten all of you killed?"

She stopped in midstride. He knew then, with awful clarity, that she had meant to throw herself into his arms, but his angry questions had stopped her cold.

"I'm sorry," she whispered, her composure crumbling, her voice trembling with aftershocks of terror and pain. "I'm so terribly sorry. I…I did it for Alan."

"You should have waited," he said more softly, in control of himself once more. "You should have waited for me."

"I waited as long as I could, Lucas," she said. "He was going to get away. I couldn't let that happen."

Vaguely he realized that Milo and Juliana had come out of the motor home, followed by Grace Winters. Several other figures had also emerged out of the darkness and the chaotic noise of the race going on around them. The race. He'd forgotten all about it for those minutes his every atom of awareness had been focused on Mattie and her assailant.

"Mattie, are you okay?" Steve Clayton shouted, moving swiftly past Winters as he was hustled into one of the track's gasoline-powered carts.

"I'm fine, Daddy," she said, letting him take her in his arms. "I'm fine."

He tipped up her chin. His expression turned dangerous and Lucas knew, if he had ever doubted it, that the former NASCAR champion was not a man to cross lightly. "You don't look fine. What happened?"

"I'll tell you all about it," she said, "as soon as I stop shaking like a leaf." Then she buried her face in his shirt and began to cry.

MATTIE LET HERSELF BE enfolded in her father's embrace. It had been so long since he'd held her like this, years and years of being at odds with each other. She was glad they were over. "Tony killed Alan, Dad," she whispered against his shirt. "He admitted it and I got it on tape."

"Good for you, honey," he said, kissing the top of her head. "But I'm getting in line right behind Lucas to give you a piece of my mind. Don't ever do anything like that again."

Mattie tried to manage a smile but knew it didn't come off right. Her face hurt and she was afraid she was going to have a black eye by morning. But the bruises on her cheek didn't hurt one-tenth as much as the bruise on her heart. Lucas had turned on her with so much anger and, worse, what she was afraid was real contempt in his eyes. She had justified his low opinion of gung-ho reporters—and in spades.

"Dad," she said. "I want to go home."

"You can't, Mattie. Not until you've given your statement." Lucas's voice was as cold as her insides. It took all the courage she had left to lift her eyes to his face. Her heart sank when she encountered the cool, emotionless stare that she had associated with him months ago.

"Do I have to go to the police station?" At the moment that seemed too much to handle.

"I think we can do it here." She didn't recognize the stern-looking black man who had materialized by Lucas's right shoulder. "Harris, track security," he said by way of introduction. "If you'll come with me, there's a Charlotte P.D. detective waiting to speak to you in my office."

Mattie nodded her acquiescence, looking around her for the first time. Grace Winters was standing at the edge of the fold-out canopy that formed a patio along the length of the motor home, her father, Dan Hunt, beside her. Stocky and broad-shouldered, the former Cargill Racing crew chief formed a contrast to Grace's slender form and shining blond hair. Dean Grosso was standing with them, and it must have been he who'd summoned Dan from the Sanford Racing pit box where Mattie remembered seeing him earlier.

Dean spoke with Grace briefly before striding over to where Milo and Juliana were sitting, hands clasped, side by side on a fold-up picnic table. Milo began talking animatedly to Dean, no doubt describing his part and Juliana's in the takedown of Tony Winters. Juliana was holding a heavy iron skillet, her weapon of choice, and one she clearly didn't intend to relinquish until Tony Winters was safely out of the way. Mattie smiled; Juliana was a woman after her own heart.

But Milo wasn't Lucas, and while the elderly gentleman gazed with pride at his wife, the love of Mattie's life was ignoring her as if she didn't exist. She felt like crying again, but wouldn't give in to the weakness.

The track official's eyes followed hers. Raising his voice, he addressed the Grossos and Grace. "I'll need statements from the three of you, too," he said.

"I need to see to my children first." Mattie didn't know Grace all that well but she could guess what was going through her mind at that moment: disbelief and betrayal and the awful knowledge that she would have to break the news about Tony to his mother and sister. Mattie did not envy her the task.

"I'll go with you to security," Steve said, putting his arm around her shoulder again. "It shouldn't take long to give your statement, and then Sarah and I are taking you home with us."

Mattie didn't have the energy to argue with him. It was kind of nice to be coddled for a change, but the fact of the matter was she had no intention of sleeping anywhere but in her own bed—so she could cry herself to sleep in private.

CHAPTER SEVENTEEN

DAWN WAS BEGINNING TO LIGHTEN the eastern sky by the time Lucas finished the paperwork required to transfer custody of his prisoner from the local cops to the NYPD. Winters, his wrist set at a local hospital emergency room, the charges pending against him in North Carolina waived in favor of the more serious ones in New York, was awaiting his fate in the local jail. Lucas would be escorting him on a flight to New York in just a few hours. He was almost in sight of the goal he'd set for himself the better part of a year earlier—solving the murder of Alan Cargill and bringing the perpetrator to justice.

But before Lucas undertook the last leg of that journey he needed to see Mattie once more, needed to know that she was all right, and that she had suffered no lasting effects from her ordeal. He parked his car in the public lot at the end of the pedestrian street he was now so familiar with. The wine shop where they had met that first afternoon was shuttered and dark, but the coffee shop next door had lights burning and the smell of baking bread was fragrant on the still air. He walked with his hands in his pockets, his shoulders hunched against the Sunday-morning chill. He wondered, briefly, who had won the race the night before. He hadn't heard, and he'd been too tired to take the time to look up the results on the Internet while he'd been waiting for Winters to be returned from the hospital.

He glanced down at his watch. Two and a half hours until the plane left for New York. Not all that much time these days, especially when you were dealing with a prisoner transfer. Maybe he should just call? The cowardly thought wormed its way past his defenses and into his consciousness. He could say goodbye just as easily over the phone. Because that was what he intended to do, say goodbye.

He'd realized something during those endless minutes that Winters had held a gun to Mattie's head. He loved her. He couldn't deny that, but beyond his feelings for her they had nothing in common, nothing to strengthen a bond that should last a lifetime. But they did have dozens of obstacles blocking their path to happiness, both large and small.

Mattie belonged here, surrounded by her friends and family and the people of NASCAR. She was part of this place, this culture. He was not and never would be.

It had all happened too fast. Ten days ago he'd barely known she existed. Now he could think of little else but keeping her safe and close by his heart. Those kinds of emotions were so rare in his life that he didn't know if he could trust they were real. He had no role model to measure them against; nothing but his parents' cold, stagnant union and his fellow cops' broken marriages. He was afraid these newfound feelings, this love, was far too fragile to last. Better to walk away now before they both ended up with broken hearts.

He almost turned back then, but something made him glance up. He saw lights burning in her apartment.

It was possible she had simply fallen asleep with them on. Or perhaps she wasn't there at all. Maybe she had taken her father at his word and gone off with him and Sarah to be fussed over and looked after for the night. He shifted his weight, angled his body to turn and walk away when he saw a figure, her figure, cross the room and pause at the window to look down directly at the spot where he stood. He took half a step back, blending into the fading night.

She stayed where she was. He felt her eyes searching the pearly darkness until they fixed on him, and held, unwavering, waiting for him to show himself. He stepped into the circle of golden light cast by an old-fashioned streetlamp, drawn by her beauty and his need to see her one last time. Their gazes locked. She motioned, making the gesture of turning a key in a lock, and disappeared from his view. He argued with himself a handful of heart beats longer and then moved into the narrow alley that ran along the side of her building. A moment later he heard the sound of a dead bolt being drawn back, a chain sliding out of its groove. The door opened and she stood silhouetted in the light at the bottom of the stairs.

"You look tired," she said, her hand curled around the half-open door.

"So do you." He reached out and touched the bruise that was already blooming on her cheek. She flinched a little, whether from pain or reluctance, he couldn't be sure and he dropped his hand to his side. "The bastard. I should have put a bullet into his brain for what he did to you."

She rose on tiptoe and touched her fingers to his lips. "Shh, don't say that. I don't want to think of you having to kill another human being, no matter how much they might deserve it."

"It's my job, Mattie. I would if I had to."

"I know." She sighed. "I know a lot more this morning than I did yesterday. I'm sorry for what I did, Lucas. I put all of us in danger because I let my heart rule my head."

"Just the way the reporter who ruined my dad's life behaved?" he asked, knowing she would recall those bitter words and take them to heart.

"No," she said, lifting her chin. "Not for the same reasons, anyway, but I ended up acting just as irresponsibly and as unprofessionally as she did. I told you I wasn't like that, but I guess I don't know myself as well as I thought I did."

"No," he said, touching her cheek with the tip of his finger. "You acted out of loyalty and love, not blind ambition and misguided zeal. The difference is as big as you can get."

"I'd like to think so." She lifted her eyes and held his gaze for a long, searching look. "It doesn't change anything between us, though."

"You're wrong there, too. It makes all the difference in the world."

She nodded. "I know. But sometimes even that isn't enough."

"You're right. Sometimes it's not." It was as close as he could come to telling her what was in his heart. It wouldn't work between them. They both knew it. Her father and mother were as bad at the marriage game as his were. They had tried and failed so many times, and Mattie had been caught in the fallout each and every time. She was as reluctant to risk her emotions as he was. It didn't matter that Steve and Sarah seemed to have "found the groove" as they said around NASCAR and were happy and content. It was too late for Mattie and him. Her scars ran deep; his did, too.

"Are you taking Winters back to New York soon?" It wasn't what he wanted to hear. What he wanted was for her to ask him to come inside, then to scoop her up in his arms and take her to her bed, make love to her.

"In a couple of hours. The Concord cops want him out of their hair as badly as I want him out of mine."

"Will you be...coming back anytime soon?" Her eyes didn't meet his this time, but seemed focused somewhere about the level of his collarbone. He had thought he could read her emotions, but not tonight. He was too damned tired, too damned confused by his own feelings to be able to decipher hers with any accuracy.

"I can't stay, Mattie," he said, knowing she would understand. "Even if I want to, I can't."

"I know that, too," she said, her eyes shining like the last of the stars winking out overhead as she blinked back tears. "And I can't go. Goodbye, Lucas. I wish you all the best." She stepped back and shut the door in his face.

"HAVE YOU SPOKEN TO LUCAS since he went back to New York?" Sarah asked. They were seated at the window of the ice-cream shop near Mattie's apartment. Sarah had called each day since Sunday to check on her. Today she had shown up in person and insisted that Mattie join her for a hot fudge sundae, which she claimed she had an intense craving for. Mattie went along with the ruse. It was better than moping around her apartment, waiting for a call from Lucas that it seemed more and more likely wasn't going to come.

"No," she said, stirring her melting ice cream with the tip of her spoon. The smells of sugar and hot fudge made her stomach lurch. It was as if she and Sarah had traded places. Her stepmother, looking healthier and happier than Mattie could ever recall seeing her, was having no problem disposing of her sweet treat.

"It's been three days since he left."

"Three days, eleven hours and twenty-seven minutes." Mattie looked up in horror. "Did I say that out loud?"

Sarah nodded. It was obvious she was trying not to smile, but the expression in her eyes showed real concern. "Yes, you did."

"Oh, God." Now she was talking to herself—and out loud to boot. She was far worse off than she'd suspected.

"Mattie, what happened after we dropped you off Saturday night? Did you and Lucas have an argument? I mean, I can't believe he didn't come by to see how you were—to talk with you..." Sarah let the sentence trail off delicately.

Mattie was glad she was wearing dark glasses to hide the bruise on her cheek; they also hid any evidence of the bruises on her heart that might show in her eyes. "He did come by. It was almost dawn but I couldn't sleep. I saw him standing right there." She pointed diagonally across the narrow brick street. "We talked." She swallowed hard against the lump of tears stuck halfway down her throat. It had been there since Sunday morning. It was no wonder she couldn't eat.

"You talked or you argued?" Sarah asked pointedly, but gently.

"We didn't argue. He said he couldn't stay. I said I understood. And he went."

"That's the abridged version, I'm guessing."

Mattie looked across the table at the woman who had been little more than a stranger for so many months but whom she now considered a friend. "No, I'm afraid it's not."

"You didn't try to stop him? You just let him go?" Sarah lifted her hand into the air in a gesture of disbelief. "Mattie, you're in love with him, aren't you?"

"I think so," Mattie whispered around the thickening lump of tears. Was it so obvious? She supposed it was.

"You think so?" Sarah repeated in a professorial tone that demanded an explanation. Mattie didn't even consider refusing. She was beginning to realize her stepmother could be a very formidable woman when she put her mind to it.

"I don't know," she repeated hopelessly. "I've thought I was in love before, and every time I turned out to be wrong. And every one of those broken romances left another crack in my heart. If I made the same mistake by falling in love with Lucas when he doesn't love me back, well, this time it will break right in two."

"I don't think you're wrong, or that it's a mistake. He's a good man. I can tell."

"It doesn't make any difference." The tears were so treacherously close that she had to stop and swallow hard to keep them in check. "He's gone and he didn't say anything about coming back."

"Of course it makes a difference." Sarah pushed her empty ice-cream dish aside. "Did he seem eager to go?"

The question caught Mattie off guard. She tried to think back to those few, wrenching minutes in the predawn of Sunday morning. She really couldn't remember what his expression had been, his body language, even then she had been battling to hide the tears that had plagued her ever since. She closed her eyes and tried again, casting her thoughts back in time, ignoring the pain, concentrating on her memories of the sound of his voice.

"He said, 'I can't stay, Mattie. Even if I want to, I can't.'"

Sarah leaned back in her chair, nodding. "He wanted to stay, Mattie. I imagine he was waiting for you to ask him to. Or at least ask him to come back as soon as he could—"

"Or for me to say I'd go to him?"

"That, too."

"How can you be sure of anything when you've barely known a person for two weeks?"

"A very intense two weeks," Sarah reminded her.

Mattie felt herself flush. The sex had certainly been intense; that went without saying. But the rest? Was it all one-sided? Was it all wishful thinking on her part? Hope flared to life inside her despite her efforts to snuff it out. "Our lives are on two separate tracks," she said, bringing up another impediment to a long-term relationship.

"If you're looking for me to tell you I believe it's best you dump the guy because distance and job commitments will doom the relationship to failure, you've come to the wrong woman. Your father and I are managing pretty well with a bicoastal relationship. I admit we're going to have some serious adjustments to make when the baby gets here, but I'm confident we'll make it all work somehow."

"You're a very confident woman," Mattie said. "I'm not so sure I have the resources you do."

"Nonsense. You're intelligent and focused and very successful at your chosen profession."

"And I have a lousy track record in the happily-ever-after department."

"That can change, too, if you want it badly enough. Your dad's a shining example. Get on a plane. Go to New York and find Lucas. Have it out with him. Tell him you love him. I bet you haven't said the words, have you?"

Mattie pushed back her chair and stood up from the table, panic nipping at her. How many times had she told herself to do just that? Go to him. Fight for what they could have together. A hundred at least, but she was still here, still alone. "I can't do that. I don't have the courage." Her voice dropped to a whisper. "I don't want to be hurt again."

If she expected sympathy from Sarah, she didn't get it. "If you don't try, you will never know what might have been," her stepmother said briskly. "And you'll regret it for the rest of your life. Mattie, think of it. The rest of your life—and his. That's a very long time to be alone."

CHAPTER EIGHTEEN

A VERY LONG TIME TO BE ALONE. Sarah's words echoed in her head for the rest of the day. Twilight was settling over her quiet neighborhood, lengthening the shadows in her living room when she couldn't stand the drumbeat of those words a moment longer. Her father had been alone for a lot of years before he met Sarah. Oh, sure, there had been the cover models and the Hollywood starlets, but there hadn't been anyone special in his life until he met and married her stepmother. Some of the endless traveling and partying must have been to mask the loneliness. Now he was a different man, working hard to make a partnership of his marriage, and a family for his new baby—and his old one.

She wanted that same kind of happiness—at least a chance at it. She wasn't a coward. She could and would fight for what she wanted, desired, needed more than anything in the world—the man she was afraid she was destined to love for the rest of her natural life, one Lucas Haines, NYPD. The details of how she would manage that feat were still up in the air, but she sure as heck was going to try. And not over the phone, either. If he didn't love her, didn't want her in his life then he was going to have to tell her to her face. Mattie grabbed a carry-on bag from her closet, threw in a change of underwear and her toothbrush and comb and headed for the door before she could change her mind. She'd camp out at the airport if she had to, until she could get a seat on a flight to New York.

She was going to find Lucas and tell him straight to his handsome face that she loved him, and demand to know in return if he loved her, too. *And if he didn't?* Well, she could always enter a convent or get a cat and become an eccentric old maid—or, more to her liking, a world-renowned, bestselling author of sports-themed novels. It didn't matter what she did as long as she kept moving, didn't let herself get cold feet and skulk back to her apartment to cry her eyes out one more time, and end up staying there, alone, for the next fifty years.

Her moment of reckoning came a whole lot sooner than she had been expecting. She shot the dead bolt at the bottom of her kitchen stairs, opened the door and took one step that propelled her directly into the arms of the man she loved. "Lucas? What are you doing here?" she blurted, wondering if she had conjured him from thin air. There were deep lines etched at the corners of his mouth. His chin was covered by three days' growth of beard. He looked as dark and dangerous as any of the criminals he dealt with—except for his eyes. His eyes held longing and the same kind of uncertainty that had held her nearly immobile for three long, weary days.

His arms came around her, held her tight. "I'm here, looking for you," he said with a grunt as the force of her impact knocked the breath out of him. "Where are you going?"

"I'm on my way to the airport to fly to New York and hunt you down," she said, her heart beating so fast she could feel it high in her throat. He was no phantom. He was warm and hard and solid as a rock. She didn't want to move, but she couldn't stay where she was, half in, half out of the doorway.

"You're on your way to New York?" The darkness left his eyes, replaced with a fierce light of triumph that warmed her from the top of her head to the soles of her feet. Her wayward courage came flooding back.

"Not anymore." Mattie dropped the handle of her carry-on and pulled him inside, shutting the door, cocooning them in the small entry at the bottom of the steps.

"I tried to stay away," he said, sliding the tips of his fingers down the side of her face, cupping her chin in his palm, "but I couldn't."

She shivered as they touched, and she thought he did, too. "I tried to convince myself it was best for both of us, too."

"A hundred good arguments, rational, well thought out—shot to hell in the middle of the night."

"Exactly," she whispered, brushing her fingers though his hair.

"I would have been here sooner," Lucas groaned, taking her into his arms for a long, drugging kiss, "but I had a lot of paperwork to fill out. God, I've missed you, Mattie," he said roughly, resting his forehead against hers. She felt his arms go around her, wrapped hers around his waist and pressed herself against him. This was where she'd wanted to be for days. This was where she belonged, in his arms, and he in hers. She closed her eyes, took a long, steadying breath. She wanted to be the one to say it first, to be the one to stop looking inward and backward at the hurts and failures of the past.

"Lucas?"

"Yes, Mattie." He was kissing her again, her eyelids, her cheek, the curve of her ear.

She bracketed his face with her hands so that their eyes were locked. "I love you, Lucas Robert Haines," she said softly.

He lifted one eyebrow slightly. "You've been on Google again, eh?"

"Yes."

"I love you, Matilda Elizabeth Clayton," he responded with a smile.

She groaned. "Oh, Lord, you know my name is Matilda."

"I do."

"But I bet you didn't know I was named for my great-great-aunt because I was born on her birthday and she was very rich. It was my grandfather's idea."

"I thought there might be some explanation along those lines. Did she leave you all her money when she died?" he asked with a wicked, teasing grin that made her knees want to fold up under her.

"She lived to be ninety-seven and she left every cent to her cat." He laughed and she laughed with him. "What else do you know about me, Lucas?" she asked, serious once more.

"I know all kinds of things about you, Mattie, love. I know you're stubborn and single-minded, loyal to your friends and a terror to your enemies. You like ice cream and fast cars and good wine. But that's only a fraction of what I want to learn about you. The rest will take me a lifetime, I suspect, so I think we should get started right away." He took her by the hand and led her up the stairs, through her tiny kitchen and into her bedroom as if he knew the way as well as she did.

"I know things about you, too, Lucas," she whispered as he took her in his arms once more. "You're honest and brave and steadfast. You never let the bad guys win. You're a good sport and a great kisser. But what frightens me a little—a lot actually, are the big things. The important things…"

He tightened his grip. "Ask away, Mattie."

"What about…marriage and babies and…?"

"Yes," he said.

"Yes?"

"I admit I wasn't ready for any of that before I met you, but I am now. Yes, to all those things, Mattie. In time. At our own pace. Deal?"

"Deal. But—"

"No more buts. Right now all I want to do is make love to you, lie beside you, wake with you in my arms and know that this is all real and not just another dream."

"You dream about me?" she asked, pleased to know he suffered from the same malady she did.

"Awake and asleep. I love you, Mattie," he affirmed once more before he pulled her down beside him on the bed. "I'm going to tell you that every day for the rest of our lives."

"And I promise never to get tired of hearing it. I love you, Lucas," she said, and went happily into his arms.

"YOU'RE AWAKE EARLY," Lucas said, coming up behind her as she sat at her desk, her laptop open in front of her.

"There's coffee in the kitchen," she said, wiggling a little in her seat as he bent to kiss the nape of her neck.

"Sounds good." He went to get himself a cup. When

he came back, she was frowning at the screen. "Anything wrong?"

"No." She hurried to explain. "Just the headlines about Tony Winters being arrested. It's still all over the news and the TV. It's going to be hard on his family. I still don't know what made him do it."

"Most honest people can't fathom what goes on in a killer's mind. He may be telling the truth. It may have been an accident. He was in way over his head with the thugs he was dealing with. He'd already skimmed tens of thousands of dollars from Matheson, probably to pay off the thugs. I wouldn't be surprised to find out he's stealing from his sister-in-law's business, too."

"I think you're right about stealing from Grace." She was quiet a moment, trying hard not to let herself relive those long, scary minutes in Juliana and Milo's motor home. "And you're right about something else, too. I don't understand what makes a person like him tick. I'm just glad he'll get what's coming to him."

"It'll blow over soon enough. Is what that bastard did to you the reason you can't sleep?" he asked in a way that made her glad Tony Winters was in jail a thousand miles away—for his sake, as well as Lucas's.

"I'm fine," she assured him, and she was, now that he was here beside her. "I just couldn't sleep any longer." She smiled. "We went to bed way too early last night."

"But we didn't go to sleep early," he reminded her with that sexy, wicked grin he reserved especially for her. "What are you doing now?"

"I'm making notes," she said, scooting her chair over to make room for him.

"Notes on what?" he asked. "Your next investigative report?"

"I guess you could call it that." Mattie lost her train of thought for a moment as he dropped to one knee beside her. He wasn't wearing anything but his jeans and another day's growth of dark beard. She found she was having trouble forming even a single coherent thought with him so close.

"'Ask D about G,'" he said, shifting his gaze from the laptop screen to look at her with narrowed eyes the color of the midnight sky. "You're back to that again?"

"It came to me this morning when I was transferring the photos from my cell phone to the computer—what 'ask D about G' might really mean."

"So now you're out here doing this when we could have been making love again?" he asked, running his finger over her collarbone and into the V-neck of her sleep shirt—the largest piece of clothing she was wearing, she realized suddenly. It wouldn't take long to rid herself of it if the opportunity should arise.

She felt herself blushing. She really didn't need to be taking notes right now, she decided. But the mysterious phrase had caught Lucas's interest. "Okay, I'll bite. Leaving Granola-Plus out of the equation and eliminating, 'ask Dean about Gina' what did you come up with?" He peered more closely at the screen. "'Ask Dan about Grace'? Okay, I suppose Alan might have meant that. 'Ask Dean about Grace?'" He gave her a hard, look. His detective look.

"Keep reading."

"'Ask Dan about Gina'? You think there's a connection between Grace Winters and Gina Grosso?"

"More than a connection, Lucas. I think Grace Winters may just be Gina Grosso."

His left eyebrow climbed slightly. "Granted, she's the right age, the right coloring, but so are a bunch of other women connected with NASCAR. Remember Becky Peters thought she was Gina Grosso, too, there for a while last summer."

"I know. I know." She toggled through a file of pictures until she found the one she wanted. "Look." It was the picture she'd taken at Grace's cooking demonstration. The one of Grace and Sophia and Patsy. "Really look at them. Do you see what I see?"

"Three women. All blond, all with the same physical build, all with the same coloring. And Grace is the right age to be Gina—well, within a few months anyway. So?"

"Their smiles," she said, triumphantly, leaning back in her chair. "Look at their smiles." She reached out and ran her finger across the screen. "So very much alike."

"And you think Winters saw the same thing you did?"

"I don't know," she said with a sigh. "There's where my intuition lets me down. He did try and deliberately delete my pictures, though. Whatever for? Other than because he thinks Grace is Gina, too?"

"If he does think she's Gina, why try and keep anyone else from finding out?" he asked reasonably.

"I wish I knew," she said, sighing. "I wish I knew."

"You're not going to figure out what the heck he was up to trying to delete that picture even if you sit there staring at the screen for the next week," he said, pulling her up out of the chair and taking her into his arms, moving them steadily back toward the bedroom. She gave one rueful look over her shoulder at the picture of the three smiling women.

"Maybe Tony stumbled across some clue to Gina's identity that we haven't picked up on," she theorized.

"Do you suppose he meant to extort money from Dean and Patsy? Make them pay to find out the truth of what happened to baby Gina?"

"Don't, Mattie. You'll only make yourself crazy wondering."

A sharp pain stabbed her heart. "Oh, God, Lucas, maybe that's the real reason he killed Alan? To keep him from telling Dean something important about Gina and Grace. Something Alan learned or remembered."

"Mattie here's the cold hard facts. Alan Cargill is dead. We will probably never know for sure what he meant by 'ask D about G.' Winters will have lawyered up by now. He won't say a word more than he already has if he has the sense God gave a duck. Sometimes the bad guys win."

"Not if I can help it," she said, narrowing her eyes. "Any good at Internet detecting, Haines?" she asked, tilting her head, sizing him up as a potential partner in her work, as well as her bed. "I'm going back over your case notes word for word. We can work this case together on the Net. Long-distance if we have to." The thought brought her down to earth in a hurry. "Lucas, when do you have to go back to New York?"

"Sometime next spring."

"What?"

They were back at her bedroom door. The bed looked rumpled and welcoming. She couldn't wait to get back in it. "I took a six-month leave of absence from the department. Didn't I tell you last night?"

"No," she said, grinning broadly, soaring high again

so quickly it made her dizzy. "It must have slipped your mind."

"A lot of things slipped my mind last night but not the most important one. I love you, Mattie." He sat down on the side of the bed and pulled her between his legs.

"I love you, Lucas, but now that you've brought it up maybe we should get one or two more things squared away before—" She waved her fingers at the bed.

"Like what, Mattie?"

"Well, your mother for one thing. When can I meet her?"

"Whenever you want. As long as it's after you've agreed to marry me. I don't want you backing out of our deal if the two of you don't hit it off."

"We'll hit it off, I promise you," Mattie said, and she meant it.

"What else do you want to discuss?"

"Where are we going to live? I mean, after the six months."

"Wherever you want. I'm thinking I might put my name in with the Charlotte P.D., or maybe strike out on my own. Start my own consulting firm. Specialize in race security, maybe?"

"Sounds good to me."

"What about you, Mattie? What do you want to do?"

"I want to marry you," she said without hesitation. "And I want to keep doing what I've been doing, at least for a while. Then maybe I'll try my hand at wine making…and baby making…. Does that sound good to you?"

He tugged her gently down onto the bed. "It sounds perfect."

"We can do this. We can make it work."

He took her in his arms and held her close. "Sure, we can. We'll just take it one day at a time…for the next fifty years or so."

* * * * *

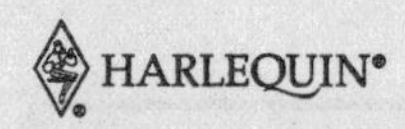

NASCAR®

Wendy Etherington
RAISING THE STAKES

When accountant Evie Winters returns home to North Carolina, she isn't prepared for the powerful reaction she has when reunited with Jared Hunt, her girlhood crush. Charged with cutting costs on his NASCAR team, Evie faces tough decisions that could cost the "engine whisperer" his job. But there's more at stake than the bottom line: this time their growing attraction might just lead to happily ever after.

Available April
wherever books are sold.

www.GetYourHeartRacing.com

NASCAR18533